Deeper Than Love

Deeper Than Love

Blake Karrington

www.urbanbooks.net

Urban Books, LLC
300 Farmingdale Road, N.Y.-Route 109
Farmingdale, NY 11735

ISBN 13: 978-1-64556-514-7

First Trade Paperback Printing August 2023
Printed in the United States of America

10 9 8 7 6 5 4 3 2 1

Distributed by Kensington Publishing Corp.
Submit Orders to:
Customer Service
400 Hahn Road
Westminster, MD 21157-4627
Phone: 1-800-733-3000
Fax: 1-800-659-2436

Deeper Than Love

by

Blake Karrington

Prologue

Steering the dark sedan into the Bank of America parking lot, the driver slowly swept his eyes over the surrounding area. Loud music resounded from a passing SUV, while to the left, a woman who looked to be in her early to mid-twenties led a small toddler in the direction of a waiting car. Locking eyes with the youngster and receiving a frown and antagonistic wag of the tongue, the driver, in any other instance, would have found this act funny. However, today was different. Ignoring the child and his mother completely, he focused on the bank and tightened the silencer on the Heckler & Koch 9 mm that sat on his lap. Then he placed his dark shades over his eyes and slowly turned to face the men sitting quietly in the sedan with him.

Watching as they screwed on their silencers, the driver—their appointed leader—replayed the plans that had been made earlier through his mind. He was prepared to carry them out and sure that his crew was as well, so he realized there was no need to cover any last-minute strategies. They had been through this too many times. Thus, in his opinion, he knew that his team was well prepared.

"Team One, everything is in order on this end!" the no-nonsense voice announced through the headset.

Breaking his train of thought, the driver glanced down at his watch. No response or reply was necessary because this particular drill had been reenacted numerous times.

"Team One, it's clear on my end as well!" A loud crackling sound could be heard through the headset after the message, making it clear to each passenger in the car that their backs were truly covered. The two vehicles that covered their getaway carried enough, if not more, ammunition and weapons than were needed to hold off a small army.

Grabbing the black gym bag beside him on the seat, the driver set the three-minute timer on his Breitling Bentley watch. Then snapping a round into the pistol chamber and placing the weapon in his waistband, he said, "You both know the routine, so let's go get this money."

Exiting the vehicle with a cocky, insistent stride, the three men could have held the titles of executive officers of any Fortune 500 company. Their Brooks Brothers suits, wingtip shoes, crisp starched white shirts, and overcoats flapping in the breeze with every forward step distinguished them from the others they passed on their short journey into the bank. Only what no one seemed to notice or care for was that the well-dressed men had come to rob them. Naturally, therefore, as they entered the bank with weapons drawn and yelling loudly, the employees and patrons were surprised.

Nevertheless, this was nothing new or out of the ordinary for the three bank robbers. Today's robbery would be the thirteenth for their crew. They were becoming a serious thorn in the side of Atlanta's law enforcement agencies. Yet, the only thing that mattered to them was the millions that were so obtainable. Thanks to their newly acquired riches, the game had suddenly changed . . .

Chapter 1

Tossing the heavy briefcase in the middle of the large oak conference table, Agent Johnson stared blankly at the surveillance photos that escaped the folder and scattered all over the heavily varnished surface.

Far removed from his normal calm, cool demeanor, Johnson was experiencing the stress that accompanied his job for the first time in his vivid memory. "Okay," he announced, blowing out a short breath, "it seems that the director has taken a personal interest in this case." Johnson continued, pointing to the folder in clear view with large portions of its spilled contents. "Since those hillbillies down South can't seem to wrap up this thing, as you're all probably aware of by now, the task has been dumped in our laps."

"So, you're telling us that between Atlanta PD and our own people down in Georgia, no one can catch and prosecute these clowns?" the junior agent questioned in disbelief as he rummaged through the photographs on the table.

"Yep. I'm afraid that's exactly what I'm telling you. However, since I'm very much aware of how enormous each of your workloads is, I've decided to send someone else down there to investigate this mess."

Raising his brows in a mixture of surprise and relief, the agent asked, "If you're not planning to send one of us—and we are your best men in the Bureau—then who could you possibly expect to get the job done?"

Noting the looks on the faces of the other agents seated around the conference table that mirrored the junior agent's words, Johnson momentarily withheld his response. Thinking that with a case of such magnitude, he honestly hoped that he hadn't made the wrong decision regarding his choice.

"Well, who's the lucky candidate?" another agent asked, snapping Johnson out of his thoughts.

"Umm, you all know—" Johnson began, only to be cut short by the sound of the conference room door opening. He turned in the direction of the door, and his magnetic glance also seemed to draw the other agents' attention to the intruder. Smiling internally, he subtly cleared his throat and stated, "Good afternoon, Agent Valentine. I'm honored that you could make it."

Unnerved by the fact that she was late, Ciara felt as if every eye in the room was staring at her and through her. Although she smiled brightly, showing no apprehension as she returned the greeting, she quickly made her way to the only empty seat in the room and quietly sat down, hoping she would no longer be the center of attention.

"All right," Johnson announced in an authoritative voice, intentionally bringing the little sideshow of sorts to an end, "seeing as though you're here, Ms. Valentine, I no longer need to explain your presence to the other agents." Winking his eye in an attempt to lighten her apparent anxiety, he received a slight trace of a smile from her before moving on.

"Now, as I was saying," he began, hardening his features as he paused to look each of the men around him in their eyes, "Agent Valentine, here, will be my eyes and ears on this one." Seeing the baffled looks around him, he turned to Ciara, not surprised to find an identical look plastered across her face as well, and stated, "The file in front of you is yours. Study it and become familiar with the circumstances of this case ASAP because your plane leaves for Atlanta at 3:00 p.m., and I want you on it."

Hearing her superior officer's words, Ciara quickly looked away from the multitude of eyes that held her with disdain. Most of her coworkers resented the fact that she had been the recent recipient of some of the top cases. A few felt it was only because she was a woman of color or double minority that checked multiple boxes. But the only thought in Ciara's mind at that moment was the envelope that her fingers were now clamped upon. However, as she began to remove the contents from within, it slowly dawned on her that after years of playing second fiddle to the other agents she had been allowed to work with, she had finally been assigned her own case. Now unable to control the smile that suddenly tugged at the corners of her mouth, she realized she had received the opportunity she'd been waiting for. Therefore, not only would she be familiar with the case and on the plane in the next two hours, but also she determined if it took every drop of strength she possessed, she vowed that she would solve the case and make a name for herself in the process.

Caught up in the file she had been studying since she left the office, the voice coming over the loudspeaker slowly registered in Ciara's mind, making her look up from the brief in her lap and listen more closely.

"I repeat, we will soon be landing at Atlanta International Airport, so at this time, all passengers must fasten their seat belts in preparation. Again, on behalf of American Airlines, I hope each of you had an enjoyable flight, and please feel free to fly with us again in the future."

Gazing out the window on her left, Ciara was immediately treated to a view of Atlanta beneath her as the plane maneuvered through the clouds in its rapid descent. Momentarily taking the time to marvel at the city's beauty from the altitude that she was witnessing it from, she closed the folder she had been peering through, placed it in the imported leather attaché case, and reached to fasten her seat belt. Flying had become second nature since she was raised as a navy brat who spent most of her childhood overseas. To her, seat belts were a necessary accessory when you were over three miles in the air and moving over 500 miles an hour or better.

Completing her last-minute adjustments, Ciara looked out the window one last time, observed the runway not too far off in the distance, and then leaned back in her seat to await the inevitable contact the plane would soon make with the tarmac. However, as the thought of one journey's end quickly exited her mind, it was instantly replaced with thoughts of the investigation she would soon embark on.

More excited now at the prospect of conquering her first solo case than when Agent Johnson had dropped the bombshell in her lap, she only hoped that her contact agent and partner in Atlanta would be as enthusiastic and professional as she was. But, sighing at the thought, she realized she wouldn't have much longer to wait until her phantom partner was revealed. They had already been assigned to bring her up to speed on the recent rash of robberies, so whoever they were, they would be waiting for her when the plane arrived.

Excited at the prospect of seeing her old friend and ex-classmate again, Sabrina scanned through the sea of exiting passengers while awaiting her first glimpse of Ciara. Though they had been tight and somewhat inseparable throughout their FBI training, upon becoming agents and between the rigors of the job and being assigned to departments in different cities, contact between them had slowly waned in the last year or so. Nevertheless, now that fate had somehow thrown the two of them back together, Sabrina saw their situation as a chance to further their reputations in the Bureau and their partnership as a means of rekindling their friendship.

Craning her neck above the scurrying crowd, Sabrina stood on her tiptoes, bringing her five foot nine height in heels to even taller proportions in her desire to catch sight of Ciara in the crowd. Then exuding a radiant smile upon seeing her girl, she quickly cleared a lane, passing through the crowd to where Ciara stood, peering off into the distance.

"If it isn't the one and only Ciara Valentine. Hey, girl," Sabrina exclaimed, noting the surprise in Ciara's bright gray eyes at the abrupt recognition.

"Sabrina! What are you doing here?" Ciara questioned, shortening the distance between them and awarding her with a hug.

Hugging Ciara tightly, Sabrina beamed joyfully, responding, "Girl, I'm here to pick you up and welcome you to my city properly. In case you haven't already figured it out, I'm your Atlanta contact. So, from this moment on, we'll be working together."

"Get out of here," Ciara laughed. "You mean to tell me that out of all the agents in Atlanta, I was lucky enough to be paired up with your crazy ass?"

She nodded with a devious smile pasted on her face and responded, "That's correct. So it's you and me against the bad guys."

"Damn," Ciara exclaimed, suddenly noticing Sabrina's attire.

"What?" Sabrina asked, following Ciara's eyes as they slowly roamed her frame.

Smirking, Ciara uttered, "If it's really you and me against the bad guys, God help us. Because if the shit happens to get hot, I'm afraid you won't be of much assistance to me in that two-sizes-too-small skirt, six-inch stilettos, and that tiny piece of material you seem to call a shirt."

"Psst, whatever," Sabrina retorted, rolling her eyes in mock anger. "There's nothing wrong with my outfit. Better yet, why am I even dignifying your foolish statement with a reply anyway?" Then reaching for one of Ciara's suitcases, she teased, "Come on here, fake Alicia Keys. I need to fill you in on a lot of things. Oh, and just so you know, our cover will be models, so I look forward to seeing your big titties and booty-licious ass pouring out of one of these outfits real soon too."

"Oh no, you don't," Ciara stated forcefully. Watching Sabrina strut off in a carefree fashion, swinging her hips provocatively, she was adamant that she would never be caught dead in such a ghettofied hoochie outfit.

Slowly realizing that this case may not have been the fairy-tale case she had previously thought it would be, she sucked her teeth, shook her head, and slowly began to follow Sabrina through the vast, packed terminal. It was suddenly apparent that she had her work cut out for her.

Ciara found nothing remotely astonishing about the Richard B. Russell Building that housed the Atlanta-based offices of the FBI. In comparison, Washington, D.C.'s J. Edgar Hoover Building all but made a mockery of the smaller structure. Nonetheless, she was painfully aware that she was far removed from the city she had grown to know and love. As she sat in the makeshift conference room surrounded by blank-faced strangers, she figured that she would make the best of an otherwise bad situation until the case she had been sent to oversee was solved.

"All right, ladies and gentlemen. Let us begin by opening the packets in front of us," the hoarse, somewhat masculine voice stated, interrupting Ciara's deep contemplation.

Snapping up her head as she reached out to grasp the packet, Ciara was taken aback at the thin, white female agent standing before them. Her elongated, feline features immediately brought forward thoughts that she resembled a panther. However, the piercing stare she seemed to hold Ciara with, along with the way she bared her teeth before speaking, gave Ciara the feeling that *she* had become the prey somewhere along the line.

Severing eye contact, the agent added, "Before we get started, in case you all haven't already been formally introduced, allow me to acquaint you with Agent Valentine. Ms. Valentine has been sent from the 'big city,' Washington, D.C., to solve the case and save the day." Grinning after her words, the gathered agents laughed at her intended humor.

Ciara smiled and nodded at the other agents, who barely acknowledged her presence. Most just went back to what they were doing. However, she did not miss the sarcasm hidden just below the surface in the agent's so-called humorous statement. Ciara made a mental note that it was apparent that her presence wasn't liked by all, so she quickly decided to steer clear of those agents at all costs.

"Okay. Now that the introductions have been made let's get down to business." Removing a long, glossy photo from her packet, she said, "This was taken during the Bank of America branch robbery, which brings their total number to a whopping thirteen in the last eighteen months in the Atlanta area alone." Allowing her voice to trail off, she added, "They have become much bolder in the last six robberies. They no longer settle for smaller cash withdrawals. That being the case, the Bureau has recently stepped up the level of importance, making their captures and arrests number one on our agenda."

Hearing the briefing but more caught up in the information she was reading in the packet, Ciara was astounded at the amount of money listed as being taken from each bank. It seemed that the last six robberies had left the vaults virtually empty. Therefore, she wasn't surprised when her quick calculations registered a net amount of $27,438,629. It was not only apparent to her that bank robbery was a lucrative profession, but it also suddenly seemed rather odd that they would reap such large sums from each of the banks listed when branches that small seldom, if ever, kept such vast amounts in their vaults.

Smiling with the weight of her first discovered clue fresh in her mind, she was willing to bet her life on the fact that the mysterious men in the surveillance photos had received inside intelligence from someone. Then that person probably alerted them when massive amounts of money would be sitting, just waiting to be plucked from the vaults.

"Excuse me, Agent Valentine, do you mind telling the rest of us what you seem to find so interesting that it has taken precedence over my briefing?"

Snapping out of her thoughts, Ciara was at a loss for words, embarrassed and pissed that she had allowed this bitch to make a mockery of her. "I was just thinking. I'm sorry." Biting her tongue to swallow her pride, she held the agent with an expressionless look, fighting the urge to cuss her country ass out. However, she quickly decided against that course of action. Instead, she made a second mental note and rolled her eyes, seeking out Sabrina in the room. She was calmed by the knowing wink she received once their eyes met.

Inhaling before giving her full attention to the agent who had self-appointed herself as her rival, Ciara realized that her stay in Atlanta would likely turn her job into an adventure.

Chapter 2

Peering out over the packed club through his two-way mirror, Dominique sipped his signature pineapple Cîroc while watching the crowd beneath him. From his perch three floors above the festivities, his office gave him a bird's-eye view of his upscale strip club, Paragon I.

Draining his drink in one swift motion, Dominique scanned the perimeter of his creation with apparent pride in his glimmering eyes. As if seeing it all for the first time, the magnificence of the décor never ceased to amaze him. The shining chrome and glass pillars situated around the glass floor supported a second balcony that was also glass, while leather couches and chrome and glass tables adorned the room. Fog machines gave the spacious club a mystical atmosphere, creating a dream-like state for the customers as the fluorescent lights danced across the chiseled, muscular bodies of the male strippers.

Scanning the faces of the females in attendance, it was apparent by their smiles, money scattered over the two elevated stages, and various forms of undress that he witnessed that they were having the time of their lives.

Inwardly smiling at the scene below him, he turned, set his empty glass on the desk, and proceeded across the large office. Passing the massive bank of television monitors that could have easily allowed him to observe the entire club from his desk, he made his way to the mirror on the opposite wall from the one he had just left. Instantly laying eyes on his favorite view out of the two clubs, he surveyed the many female strippers under his employment in various stages of undress.

Unlike the décor of Paragon I, its sister club, Paragon II, was decorated in gold and glass. Cages hung from the ceiling with exotic dancers moving provocatively inside, out of reach of the eager, lustful customers. Employing the most beautiful strippers in the city, Dominique held a level of pride in the realization that except for the Gentlemen's Club, no other club in the city could begin to rival his where the women were concerned.

Dominique had revolutionized the strip club industry, unlike any other club in Atlanta. Club Paragon was the only strip club in the city that catered to everyone. Thanks to innovative thinking, Paragon's ability to provide male strippers for women and female strippers for men quickly established it as a true competitor. Thanks to Atlanta's elite and all the hustlers spending their dough in the two clubs with no regard whatsoever, he had become richer than he could have ever imagined two years before when he opened the doors for business.

Knocking lightly, Sue leaned into the slightly open door. "Dom, can I have a moment of your time, please?"

Turning toward his assistant's distinct Asian accent, Dominique waved his hand, beckoning her to enter. Then displaying a grin at the sight of the exotic beauty, he strolled across the office and sat on the edge of his desk.

"I hope I'm not interrupting you or anything," she began, sitting in front of her boss and placing a fresh drink on his desk.

"No, love. My office and time are always free when you need either. So, what can I do for you this evening?" he asked, reaching for his drink and thinking that the way her Capri pants hugged her thighs and hips, he could most *definitely* accommodate her.

"Uh . . . um . . ." Sue loudly cleared her throat, garnering Dominique's attention. Smiling at the lingering look he had given her, as much as she would have loved to go a few rounds with him, after damn near experiencing a nervous breakdown behind his ass once before, the last thing she wanted to do was travel the road of heartbreak again. It had taken her several months and two different therapists to get past her near-nervous breakdown and back to work.

Returning her smile, Dominique winked his eye and said, "Go ahead," as he smoothly raised his drink to his lips.

Shaking her head more to clear her senses than in response to his antics, she said, "I need to get your signature for these liquor licenses. Also, a representative of the Hawks basketball team has been trying to reserve Paragon II next Saturday night for a private party."

Raising his brow at her last statement, Dominique realized that the party would bring major dough to the club and the strippers. However, to close the club on a Saturday night would mean that many of their regular customers would have to migrate to the club's competition. "The signatures won't be a problem, but return the team representative's call and decline the offer. We can't oblige them on such a large request, but when their team members come to the club, supply them with complimentary champagne and lap dances."

"I agree," Sue announced. "Saturday nights are our most lucrative nights, and shutting down the club isn't an option. But if I can get them to agree to settle for the VIP rooms instead, I'm going to grab that NBA money." Then tossing the invoices on the desk, she stood and headed toward the door. "I'll come back and get those later.

Right now, I have two clubs that need to be run, so have those invoices signed and ready when I return."

"Sure thing, Ms. Chan," Dominique laughed while shaking his head at the authority in her voice and the sway of her hips and ass as she sashayed out the door. "Damn," he declared, mentally reminiscing on how tender and sweet her pussy used to be. Then quickly burying any thoughts he had begun to rehash, he concluded that she had become an asset to Paragon that he wasn't willing to lose. Therefore, if tender ass were all she meant to him, he would reluctantly stick to his "hands-off the employees" policy before he jeopardized the working relationship they had achieved.

Breaking his train of thought at the loud and abrupt entrance of his best friend and business partner, Tremaine, Dominique rose from his desk and grinned at the look etched on his man's face. "What?" he asked, averting his eyes from the questioning stare that Tremaine had fixed him with.

"Yeah, you took the words right out of my mouth, my nigga," Tremaine stated, taking a swig from the champagne bottle he held. Then lowering the bottle and swallowing the liquid, he slurred, "I couldn't help noticing the smug grin pasted on Sue's face when we collided in the hallway. You wouldn't be hitting that again, by any chance, would you?" Raising his brow in a teasing manner, he added, "I can't say that I'd blame you, as fine as she is, but I could have sworn that you said the employees were off-limits, and you know you damn near put her in a mental institution last time."

"I did say that, and yeah, I know, nigga, but for your information, we strictly handle business now—unlike your ass who insists on creeping around here with all the strippers against my wishes." Giving his man a knowing wink, Dominique held Tremaine with a stern glare while holding back the smile that threatened to erupt at any moment.

"Um, so you say, huh?" Tremaine nonchalantly replied, then took another swig from the bottle. He smacked his lips as if he had never tasted anything that could begin to rival what flowed freely down his throat. Then quickly changing the subject, he said, "I made my rounds through both clubs on the way up, and as usual, there was standing room only. They're poppin' like crazy. Damn."

"Yeah, I know," Dominique responded. Smiling at Tremaine's excited outburst, he found it odd that even now, as wealthy as they were, his friend still could retain such an extreme level of enthusiasm over something as trivial as a packed house.

"Yo, I caught up with Pimp, Treon, and Money in Raw Cuts down on Peachtree earlier. Niggas said they were gonna roll up in Club Kaya tonight and make a little noise. Since everything is in order around here, how about we join them for a night out on the town?"

Taking a moment to decide, Dominique figured he would only be in the way if he hung around Paragon. Sue basically ran the clubs single-handedly, anyhow. Not to mention, he relished any opportunity he received to roll with his crew.

"So, what's it gonna be, Dom? We about to shine on these lames tonight, or what?" Tremaine questioned, wearing his customary careless grin.

"Fuck it. It's on," Dominique stated, glancing down at his Baume & Mercier watch. Though his attire was already official, it was an unwritten rule that whenever he was in the company of ballers—and many would be in attendance at Club Kaya—he made it a point to pull out all the stops. Judging by the time, it was clear that he could sign the invoices for Sue, make it home for a quick shower and a change of clothes, and still be on the runway in more than enough time for the ghetto-glamorous fashion show.

"Okay. If we're rockin' like that, then let's get it poppin'," Tremaine announced, removing his phone. "I'm gonna call up the crew and tell them we're coming through."

"Cool. Let them know we got to shoot out to Stone Mountain first. I got to get fly."

Unconsciously allowing his eyes to roam over his man's frame, Tremaine frowned and exclaimed, "Nigga, please. Damn, Dom. You're already dressed, nigga."

Staring down at his crisp Hermès button-down shirt and tailored Hugo Boss suit that kissed the tips of his suede and leather Gucci loafers just right, Dominique smirked and remarked, "For once in your life, you're right. But right or not, I've got to go home and change and wipe off my balls. You know bitches hate sweaty nuts. And if I do that, I can't put the same clothes back on, so, nigga, just relay the message."

Shaking his head, Tremaine released a short breath and began to punch a series of numbers into his phone. Though his face registered a look of annoyance, he was far from angry. This was Dominique's routine, and in all actuality, each crew member had come to understand his ritual of sorts. However, being friends with Dominique longer and sharing a closer bond, Tremaine had become accustomed to his man's pretty-boy demeanor. Concluding that he was too set in his ways to change after carrying it in the same manner for over thirty years, Tremaine inwardly smiled and disregarded the thought altogether. He strolled to the opposite side of the massive office at the sound of Treon's voice as it flowed coolly through the receiver.

Mouthing the words to T.I.'s "What You Know" thundering through the speakers, Dominique swayed his head to the rhythm. Now that he had decided to hit

Club Kaya, the anticipation was suddenly overwhelming, making it hard to concentrate on signing the invoices. However, they were a necessity, so regardless of his plans, duty called, and work, to him, was first and foremost.

Sliding the last invoice onto the already-signed pile in the center of his desk, he placed his special monogrammed gold-encrusted pen into its velvet box, sighed, and stood up. Observing Tremaine across the room as he finished his conversation, Dominique decided that tonight, he would leave any baggage that usually hindered him from letting his hair down, so to speak, behind. Burdensome relationships, hating babies' fathers, business, and any other problems would be left behind. Tonight, he planned to exude the legendary charm that had made him the toast of the city.

Heading toward the door and the night's festivities that awaited him, his last thought on the issue before exiting the office was, *The haters and lust-hungry ladies in attendance had better be prepared. I, the arrogant, conceited Dominique known for breaking hearts and backs, will soon enter the arena.*

Chapter 3

Blinking to bring some semblance of normal sight and order back to her tired, bloodshot, gray eyes, Ciara removed her reading glasses, exhaled, and slowly rubbed her aching temples in a circular motion. After scanning countless files containing miniature piles of bank robbery reports and witness statements, she found herself no closer to solving the case she had been sent to wrap up in Atlanta over a month before. She'd taken the phrase "overtime" to another dimension. Except for showers, meals that could scarcely be called meals at all, and the occasional catnap, her time in the A had been spent hard at work.

Her life would seem unusual for the average individual who lived a normal nine-to-five with two kids, a husband, a house with a white picket fence, and a dog existence. However, the life of an avid workaholic was the only life she had ever known. To live any other way than she had become accustomed to would be unrealistic as far as she was concerned.

Twisting her neck to relieve the crook that had begun to form, Ciara sighed lightly and placed her glasses back over her eyes. Unfortunately, there was no time to rest when she may have overlooked something in the sea of paperwork. With that thought in mind and a burning desire to reconstruct the pieces to the puzzle that would find the culprits she sought, she began scouring through the files in search of the one minuscule clue that she knew had to be hidden within.

Snapping up her head, the ringing phone and its unwelcome interruption instantly broke into her thoughts. Wanting to ignore it but knowing that the call could be important, she reluctantly reached for the receiver. "Hello," she said while still keeping her eyes on the report in her hand.

"Hey, girl," Sabrina yelled into the receiver, "what it do?"

"*What it do?* Come on, Sabrina. Where do you get all these ghetto terms from?" Ciara teased. "That shit already sounds corny, but coming from a federal agent, it *really* sounds ridiculous."

"Yeah, yeah. Would you please spare me the perfect English speech? Loosen up sometimes, will you? You're not a federal agent twenty-four hours a day. Then again, I forgot who I was talking to." Breaking into a fit of laughter, Sabrina added, "By the way, when was the last time you experienced an orgasm? And for the record, self-induced climaxes *don't* count."

Smiling at her girl's attempt at humor, Ciara said, "Apparently, you did forget who the hell you were talking to because not only am I an agent twenty-four hours a day, but I'm also in the middle of doing something you should be doing . . . working! And for the record, it's none of your business when I received my last orgasm, manually or otherwise. Now, how about you tell me what it is that you're calling me at . . . um . . . 9:40 at night for?" she asked, intently eyeing her watch.

"Girl, 9:49 on a Saturday night is early. And to answer your question, I'm calling to inform you that we're going out for a night on the town, Ms. Thang."

"A night out on the town? Are you *serious?* Sabrina, I'm swamped with work, and—" she began to argue. However, her reasoning was quickly cut short by Sabrina's response.

"Work, work, work. Not tonight, Ms. Valentine. You've turned me down for every invitation I've extended ever since you arrived. But just so you understand, I'm not taking 'no' for an answer tonight. Your funny-acting ass is going out with me, and that's all there is to it. Now, do I make myself clear?"

Noting the firm, no-nonsense tone of Sabrina's voice, Ciara found it virtually impossible to resort to her usual excuses for not being able to accept her girl's invitation. At a loss for any other response, she mumbled, "My hair is a mess, and what could I possibly find to wear at such short notice?"

"Girl, I know you got something in your closet that you can put on, and if not, I will bring you something super sexy, and as for the messy hair complaint . . . Come on, Ciara. Your high-yellow ass could easily chop off a foot of that shit, and it would *still* fall halfway down your back." Sucking her teeth, Sabrina remarked, "If having a long mane of silky curls is your definition of a 'mess,' I'd give anything to be messed up as well."

Deciding that any further attempts at arguing were futile, Ciara accepted defeat. "Okay, I get the point, Sabrina. Now, do you mind telling me where we're going so I can find something appropriate to wear?"

"I can't say. It's a surprise. But I will tell you this much . . . Where we're heading, some of the city's wealthiest, most eligible bachelors will be present."

The sound of excited anticipation was evident in Sabrina's reply, creating an aura of mystery that Ciara found impossible to ignore. "Sabrina, I'm hardly looking for a man, whether he's eligible or otherwise," she stated in a matter-of-fact tone.

"That I can believe." Laughing, Sabrina disregarded her comment and added, "Just let your hair down, throw on something revealing, and let me worry about our destination. I'll see you in an hour. And, Ciara, please, be ready."

Hearing the phone go dead, Ciara looked at the receiver in her hand and slowly lowered it to the bedside table. Reluctant to leave the solitude of her hotel room, it suddenly dawned on her that she hadn't experienced any semblance of nightlife in years. Except for working toward furthering her career, men had pretty much been placed on the back burner, making it easier to concentrate on reaching her long-range goal of becoming a federal agent. That being the case, any thought of meeting and finding interest in the opposite sex had basically dwindled.

However, now that she had been forced, in so many words, to step out of her self-imposed cocoon, she decided that she might as well make the best of an opportunity that didn't arise every day. So, with an hour at her disposal, she took a deep breath and stood to begin the rigorous task of recreating herself. Before it was over, she planned to turn what the reflection in the mirror defined as an ordinary FBI agent into a diva that would not only receive the utmost attention but also *command* it.

Pulling up in front of the Downtown Peachtree Plaza Hotel, Sabrina brought the sleek, silver Jaguar XK8 to a screeching halt. Radiating her signature Colgate smile due to the pleasure she received each time she sat behind the wheel of the expensive, powerful sports car, she mused that maybe one day she would genuinely be fortunate enough to own one herself. However, at that moment, thanks to whoever the drug dealer was that the government had confiscated her dream car from, she was now frontin' in style.

Smiling at the thought as her eyes sought out the dash clock, she grabbed her cell phone and speed-dialed Ciara. With no time to waste, she figured that if Ciara had followed her instructions and dressed speedily, they could be in Club Kaya, partying in no time flat. Only as she heard the frustration in Ciara's voice when she answered, it slowly began to register that they would be late.

"Come on, Ciara," Sabrina called out, staring at the closed door with a look of annoyance. Slumping back against the floral print sofa, she glanced at her watch and added, "I called you over two hours ago, which gave you more than enough time to get ready. Now, thanks to your slow ass, we'll arrive late and have to stand in a long line."

The bedroom door slowly opened, and Sabrina's vexation instantly changed into utter surprise. The picture Ciara presented before her was nothing short of phenomenal. As if seeing her girl for the first time, she was momentarily at a loss for words. Yet, even the shy, somewhat uncomfortable look pasted on Ciara's features could not deter her from the splendor that had transformed her. Smiling, Sabrina was no longer angry that Ciara had kept her waiting. On the contrary, the extra time had only assisted her friend in making herself a stunning creation.

"So, how do I look?" Ciara asked and bit her bottom lip apprehensively.

"Well . . . um . . ." Sabrina began, searching for the right words to define the magnitude of Ciara's beauty.

"Well . . . um, *what?*" Ciara screeched. Her voice increased by several decibels. "I knew this outfit wouldn't look right on me," she ranted, oblivious to the stare of disbelief Sabrina had fixed upon her.

She can't be serious, Sabrina thought, rolling her eyes at Ciara's frantic display of insecurity. As beautiful as Ciara was, it was beyond Sabrina's understanding that she could honestly be so unaware of what she possessed. Never in a million years would Sabrina have believed that Ciara could be this naïve had she not witnessed it herself.

"That's it. I'm not going," Ciara announced, shaking her head in despair. "This dress is too tight, and I refuse to go out looking like a fool." Wrapping her arms protectively around herself, she wore a look of frustration.

Bursting into loud, convulsive laughter, Sabrina shook her head, trying through gasps to form the words. "You . . . have to . . . be joking, right?" Questioning her with tears in her eyes, she said, "Your outfit is the bomb. You look gorgeous. And although your dress is rather tight, God knows you're wearing the hell out of it." Raising her brow teasingly, she added, "Honestly, I don't know whether to compliment your ass or roll my eyes and hate that you will more than likely steal my shine, girl."

Relinquishing her previous frown and giggling at Sabrina's words, Ciara's features suddenly carried a smile. Then still searching for a little more assurance, she asked, "Are you *sure* I look all right, Sabrina? I haven't been out in an eternity, and I can't ever recall showing this much skin."

"Of course, I'm sure," Sabrina declared. "You not only look fabulous, but you also do Marc Jacobs a disservice by wearing his dress so well and not modeling it for him beforehand. Not to mention, Bottega Veneta couldn't have had the slightest idea that those boots were made to be worn by you—and *only* you."

"Okay. I think I get the point. Thanks to you, my head may be a little swollen now." Ciara smiled. "But I appreciate your mental boost." Smoothing her dress down and grabbing her matching Bottega Veneta purse, she exhaled and said, "I guess I'm ready after all."

"Well, it's about time," Sabrina said, quickly rising from the couch. "I'm ready to get my party on, and Club Kaya awaits us. So come on before you change your mind again and make me later than I already am."

Waving her hand toward the door, Ciara said, "Lead the way. After how you gassed up my head, against my better judgment, I think I'm ready to get my party on as well." Returning Sabrina's grin, she winked her eye, presenting a false picture of strength and excitement when her initial nervousness still existed. However, as they headed out the door, she made a silent oath to try her best to make the most of their night out on the town. Although it would all be new to her due to her work, work, and more work-related lifestyle, tonight, Ciara planned to take Sabrina's earlier advice.

Removing the clasp that held her soft, satiny tresses in place, she shook her head, allowing her hair to swing free. Then inwardly smiling at the bigger picture of her action, the realization struck her that now that she had, in fact, let her hair down, she only hoped that she wouldn't regret her decision to do so.

Chapter 4

"Well, as usual, you've made us late with that pretty-boy shit. Damn, Dominique. Why you always got to pull this last-minute shit?" Tremaine complained in his usual, fed-up tone.

Dominique's only reply was a soft laugh. He'd heard this argument, and many others, from Tremaine through the years. However, as they traveled I-20 whipping in and out of traffic, his mind whirled with memories of traveling the same path over a decade ago. It was that moment in the past that Atlanta and all of its splendor was revealed to his young, dream-struck eyes . . .

Twelve Years Earlier

"There it is, youngster," the old man beamed, never taking his eyes off the bright skyline that loomed ahead. "That there is Atlanta, the greatest city in the South. I tell you, a Black man can surely find his fortune there."

Flicking his eyes from the excited face of his old traveling companion to the vast, lit structures that stood only mere miles ahead, Dominique couldn't control the nervous energy that increased his already steadily beating heart. After the lengthy trip, he was finally here. Atlanta, Georgia, his lifelong destination, was indeed before his eyes.

"Youngster, what are your plans once we reach the Greyhound Bus Terminal? If you need any help finding anything, I'm the man to ask." The old man proudly made the announcement, removing the tattered fedora he wore in what seemed to be a gracious gesture. "Don't hesitate to call on me," he reiterated, replacing his hat and tearing his bright eyes away from Dominique.

"I . . . " I won't," Dominique stuttered, realizing that he had no immediate plans. The hardest part had been working and saving every dollar he could to come to the city named the "Black Mecca." Now that he was here, besides the clothes he wore, a few articles that he carried in the tattered suitcase in the compartment above his seat, and several hundred dollars that lined his otherwise lint-covered pockets, he found himself in a big city with no family or friends.

Excited at the prospect of the unknown, a smile slowly began to form upon his smooth, chocolate features. At that moment, he did not doubt that he would make it. Regardless of what barriers awaited, the young man who hailed from a small town in Virginia would find his fortune by whatever means were at his disposal . . .

The increased speed of the Ferrari as it veered on the exit ramp, along with Tremaine's recital of the words to Young Jeezy's "R.I.P.," brought Dominique back to the present. Cutting his eyes in the direction of his best friend and brother by another mother, the fleeting glance of love and admiration was quickly shortened as the blaring horns, and loud music from the traffic captured his attention.

"Okay," Tremaine stated loudly. His eyes were glued to the sea of dime pieces and dime-piece wannabes that pranced past the slowly moving sports car. Whistling and winking at the scantily clad booty-licious stallion that waved and blew a kiss in return, he grinned and said to himself, "I love this shit."

Dominique smiled at his man, ignoring the wanting looks trained in their direction from the passing females. Tremaine was in superstar mode, and Dominique was highly aware of that. As for himself, he realized that the forest-green Ferrari convertible sporting twenty-inch Antera spinners and peanut butter interior quickly gave the lamest dudes the ability to be pussy magnets. He found it more challenging to meet and conquer women through conversation, not material objects that easily garnered the attention he knew his words and actions could solely achieve on their own accord.

Catching sight of their friends parked directly in front of the club, Dominique said, "Hey, Don Juan. When you take a break from soaking up all the attention, how about pulling over there where the rest of your pussy-chasing companions are?"

Tremaine's smile instantly intensified as he followed Dominique's index finger to the spot where his partners in crime were located. The women who happily gathered around the exquisite whips that Pimp, Money, and Treon drove were just Tremaine's type. They were materialistic, ghetto, and sported thick, sexy bodies that the Georgia Peach State was renowned for. With that thought in mind, he ignored Dominique's comment in his haste to join his so-called "pussy-chasing" partners.

"Um . . . Who is that there, girl?" one of the young gold diggers asked, poking her thick, glossy lips out in a pouty manner. The excitement in her eyes and tone of voice garnered the glances of the women standing close to her.

"Damn, that Ferrari is hot as shit. Who does that whip belong to?" another gawking chick asked, stepping away from the chromed-out Porsche Cayenne truck and driver who had completely held their attention before the Ferrari's appearance.

Frowning, Money threw his hands up in annoyance as he too wondered who the hell was pushing the attention-grabbing whip. Of course, the booming sounds of the Jay-Z and Rick Ross remix of "Fuck With Me, You Know I Got It" wasn't helping matters either as the new arrivals quickly stole his, Treon, and Pimp's shine.

Rising off his Mercedes CLS 5 Series hood, Treon lifted his Prada shades and squinted his weed-reddened eyes toward the Ferrari that had grasped everyone's attention throughout the packed parking lot. From his peripheral view, he witnessed Pimp, who was parked beside him in the convertible BMW 645, as he too cut short the conversation he was having with a young hottie to see who it was that had the crowd in an uproar.

Enjoying the females' lustful stares and the jealous glares that numerous haters shot their way as they crept through the parking lot, Tremaine was in his element. His patronizing grin was the opposite of the solemn look that sat upon Dominique's features. Nevertheless, even though Dominique had more control over his emotions than his friend did, he too was feeling the grandeur of their late arrival. Even if he hadn't shared the reason behind his always waiting until the last minute to get dressed and on his way to whatever affair they chose to frequent, it basically came down to the fact that he loved to make a late, grand entrance.

"Oh, hell nah." Money was the first to identify the passengers of the sleek sports car as they pulled up beside his truck and shot him knowing smiles.

"We should have known," Treon and Pimp said in unison.

However, Treon passed Tremaine the blunt of dro (hydro) he had been smoking and reached inside the Ferrari to grab the bottle of Patrón that sat between the front seats. "Park this shit, and let's get our party on," he said, drinking straight from the bottle.

Ready to do precisely what Treon had suggested, Dominique agreed and got out of the car before Tremaine parked in front of Pimp's BMW. Giving each of his partners pounds and brotherly hugs, he looked past the flirtatious stares directed at him from the many women surrounding them. Instead, he found himself surveying the long line and gawking females who were gazing in his and his friends' direction

"Excuse me. My name is Gina, and I hate to impose, but aren't you the owner of Club Paragon? I think I auditioned for you before."

Hearing the voice that carried the familiar Southern twang he had become accustomed to, Dominique could not answer her or, for that matter, turn around. His eyes were locked upon those of a woman in line who held him in a mysterious trancelike grip. Hating to blink for fear that their connection would be broken even through the constant rambling of the female behind him, he felt drawn to the splendidly beautiful specimen before him for reasons unknown to himself.

"Yo, Dom, what's up? You a'ight over there, nigga?" Tremaine called out, drawing his attention away from the mystery woman for a split second.

"Yeah . . . um . . . I'm good," Dominique responded. However, as he turned back to search for the woman who had held his interest, she was no longer there. Frantically scanning the crowd in search of her but finding her nowhere, he sighed and concluded that he was trippin'. Turning to join his crew, he decided that there were too many women in and around Club Kaya to be sweating one, especially a mystery one.

Chapter 5

"Ciara . . . *a-hem*," Sabrina cleared her throat loudly, attempting to get her girl's attention. "Excuse me, but are you coming in or what?"

Blinking to clear her head, Ciara replied, "Huh? I'm sorry. I was just looking at . . ." Noticing the strange look her friend was giving her, she cut her response short. On second thought, she decided it would be advantageous to keep her thoughts to herself.

Slightly rolling her eyes as she sucked her teeth, Sabrina said, "Come on, girl. You're holding up the line, and regardless of whether you realize it, the people behind you aren't too happy about it."

Shooting a glance over her shoulder, Ciara mumbled, "Oops, I'm sorry," in response to the angry scowls she witnessed on the faces of the annoyed clubgoers in line behind her. Peering off into the parking lot one last time, she momentarily held eye contact with the handsome stranger who, for some reason, piqued her interest before hurrying through the doors of the club.

Following Sabrina through the club, she couldn't control her wandering mind. It was only an aspect of her speculative personality that when her interest was piqued in any way, her thirst for answers needed to be quenched. Thus, the questions reappeared: *Who is the mystery man? Is he a famous person? Maybe a professional athlete or rapper? Could he be a criminal or one of the many ballers from around the country that flock to Atlanta?*

Losing enthusiasm at the realization that the tall, chocolate dream she had just laid her eyes upon might merely
be another drug dealer, Ciara's shoulders slumped
slightly. But, curious still, she understood that although
she would probably never know who he was or what his
profession was, her own profession would never allow
her to deal with a criminal by any means. Before anything
else, she lived and breathed the Bureau. Nothing was
placed above her oath to protect and serve. *Everything*
was second to her job.

Somewhat tipsy, Ciara nursed her third cosmopolitan
of the night as she swayed to the sounds of T.I. Although
she couldn't necessarily understand what the hell he was
saying, his sexy voice rapping, *"What You Know About
That,"* definitely made her want to know about whatever
the hell he had to offer.

Turning up her drink, she giggled at the combination
of her last thought and just how ugly the lame dude
Sabrina was talking to was. It was bad enough that he
resembled Flavor Flav, but he actually had the nerve
to wear a busted outfit and a pair of scuffed, run-down
shoes.

Barely able to keep her drink down as she exploded in
laughter, Ciara could only shake her head and hunch her
shoulders in response to the evil look Sabrina gave her.

The Flavor Flav lookalike grinned in a manner that
said, *"I know you wish I would have hollered at you
first."*

Nevertheless, Ciara was just glad his ugly ass didn't
actually speak the words. If he had, there was no doubt in
her mind that all hell would have broken loose.

Concluding that she was a little more than tipsy, Ciara
set down her empty glass and swept the club with her

eyes attempting to spot one of the many waitresses. It was time for another drink; this time, her taste buds needed an apple martini.

"What it do, mama? How about letting me take you out on the dance floor?"

Turning to get a better look at the bothersome person who had invaded her space without the slightest invitation or proper greeting, Ciara could not conceal her irked expression. Smiling deviously, she allowed the alcohol to answer for her. "*What it do, mama?*" she repeated in disgust. "First of all, I only understand proper English, and I'm hoping your mama isn't in here." Then for emphasis, she glanced around her as if looking for his mother.

Glaring at Ciara through angry eyes, the guy stated, "Fuck you, you stuck-up-ass bitch! You ain't all that no damn way."

As she watched him stalk off, Ciara's mouth hung open. She would have been upset by such a disrespectful comment any other time, but tonight, she found the whole thing amusing.

"Ciara, are you okay, girl?" Sabrina asked with concern evident in her tone.

"I'm fine. Really, it was nothing." She smiled and stood up from her seat in one fluid motion. Winking her eye to calm any anxiety her friend may have had behind her dilemma, she added, "I'm going to refill my drink and visit the ladies' room."

"Would you like for me to come along?" Sabrina asked, pushing her chair away from the table.

"No. Please. Really, there's no need for that. I'll be just fine," she tossed over her shoulder, waving her hand in a gesture that signaled for Sabrina to stay seated as she headed toward her destination.

***

Between worrying about her friend and increasingly losing interest in her lackluster conversation with Mr. No Name, Sabrina's attention had all but been redirected. She didn't have the slightest clue about whatever the hell he was saying.

As her eyes traversed through the crowded club, Sabrina did a double take, nearly knocking over her drink in her haste to stand. She could hardly believe her eyes. In her view stood a ghost from her past. Seeing him instantly changed her plans for the evening. "Excuse me," she said, leaving the table and her guest behind. Excuses aside, she honestly couldn't have cared less whether her boring companion—or drink sponsor, which was a better title—was bothered by her abrupt escape.

Shouldering her way through the packed dance floor, she never took her eyes off her target. Even from a distance, his radiant smile and bright green eyes had her salivating. Yet, his tall, almond-complexioned muscular frame packed inside of an expensive designer outfit truly mesmerized her. It was crazy that after six years of no contact between them, Tremaine still possessed the power to make her heart flutter like a lovestruck teen.

Only mere feet separated her from her first and most memorable love, so taking a deep breath to calm her rapidly beating heart, Sabrina reached out to grasp his arm. Making contact with the hard, bulging muscles beneath his shirt, she swallowed the lump in her throat. She watched as his bald head slowly turned to see who had intruded on the conversation he was already engrossed in with another enchanted female.

Upon seeing whose hand held his arm, instant recognition showed on his face. The astonished look he wore said more than any words ever could. However, the excited way he pronounced "Sabrina" as he reached

down to scoop her up into his massive arms proved just
how good it felt to see her again.

Smiling brightly as she held on to Tremaine tightly
and exalted in his embrace, Sabrina received a hidden
joy from the twisted look of disgust that the female he
had been talking with before her arrival tossed her way.
Then making a face of her own that rivaled that of the
aggravated woman, Sabrina's smile broadened when
the female angrily stormed off.

Gently massaging his smooth, bald head, it was apparent by the way he stared into her eyes and shook his head
that Tremaine liked what he saw. And with that knowledge at her disposal, it was just as apparent to Sabrina
that she would soon be receiving some of the goodies that
had been absent from her life for some time now.

Chapter 6

"Yeah, I hear you, partner. But Saturdays are out of the question, my man. Believe me, if it were any other day, it wouldn't be a problem," Dominique announced, explaining to a member of the Atlanta Hawks basketball team why their request to reserve Paragon II for a private party would have to be denied.

"Psst," the platinum-and-diamond-draped basketball player sighed in disgust. "I feel where you're coming from, Dominique. Really, I do. But your joint is the hottest spot in the city. Yo, if it's about the guap (money), say the word, and we'll pay you whatever." The ice in his grille sparkled with the smile that tugged at his handsome, juvenile features after his halfhearted plea.

"Guap has absolutely nothing to do with it, and you know it. That was a good try, though," Dominique said, returning the young man's smile.

At that moment, he saw Tremaine hoisting a young lady in the air and spinning her joyously around. This was far from how his man acted toward any female. The scene caught him entirely off guard. This and the fact that the young lady looked somewhat familiar garnered his attention momentarily. "Um, I, uh . . . can't help you this time," he said, attempting to bring the conversation to an abrupt end. "But holler at me the next time you're in the club, and I'll be sure to make it worth your while. I gotta roll out, but keep it pimpin', ya heard?" Giving the younger man a pound, he headed through the crowd, evading the numerous women who attempted to halt his forward progress.

The closer he got to the pair, the more familiar the woman in Tremaine's arms became. However, no sooner than Tremaine stood her back upright and her face was clearly in view that Dominique understood why Tremaine was acting so unlike himself. Sabrina had returned.

Not wanting to intrude on the pair due to their long overdue reunion and in no hurry to return to the VIP room where the rest of his team was setting it out for an array of overly anxious females, he decided to make his way to the bar and refresh his drink. In the process, he figured that if he was lucky, his mystery woman might cross his path. Even more so than any drink or need to escape his fun-loving partners, he had found himself thinking about nothing but seeing her again since laying eyes on the unknown female. So now, he concluded that if luck was on his side, seeing her was something he would have the pleasure of doing before the end of the night.

After avoiding numerous attempts at conversation by Jheri-curled-sporting wannabe pimps, an array of gold-tooth-having street pharmacists, and an old man who could have easily gone to school with her father, Ciara was finally leaving the bar with not one but two martinis.

Sipping one of her drinks as she made her way back through the crowd toward their table, she felt a hand grasp her backside. Quickly jerking around in her haste to catch the culprit who had been bold enough to grab her ass, she spilled one of the martinis on her designer dress. "Shit," she huffed angrily.

Looking down at her ruined Marc Jacobs original, out of nowhere, it dawned on her that she was drunk. The slurring sound she had heard when she cursed clarified the issue for her. Only like the singer, Ciara would say, she too thought, *So what?* as she drank the remainder of her drink and continued.

Damn, she thought, looking around when she reached their table and found it empty. Then sweeping her eyes at a 360-degree angle, she observed Sabrina wrapped in the arms of one of the prettiest red niggas she had encountered since coming to Atlanta. He was fine as hell if light-skinned men were her preference, but Ciara's taste had always lingered more on the darker side. She liked her men the same as she liked her coffee . . . without cream.

Sweeping her eyes around the club once more with the thought of how she liked her men and not finding who she was searching for, she closed her eyes and instantly conjured up the picture embedded in her mind. Her milk chocolate dream was meticulously dressed, too damn fine, with just the right height and weight to dominate her in all the delicious ways she had been lacking for too damn long. Leaning her head back, she felt a heat slowly beginning to creep into her loins.

"Ciara, I want you to meet a very special old friend."

Snapping out of her deep contemplation at Sabrina's cheerful voice, Ciara quickly sat upright and shook off any semblance of her prior alcohol-induced haze.

"Girl, this is my old boo-boo, Tremaine." Sabrina introduced him with a lowered, lust-filled gaze in her eyes that was unmistakable.

"Hello, Ciara. It's nice to meet you," he said, extending his hand in a gentlemanly fashion.

"Likewise." Grasping his hand in a firm shake, Ciara instantly took a liking to him for some reason. Manners were always a true sign of a winner as far as she was concerned. Smiling graciously, she kindly released his hand.

"Well, Ciara, I hope we have another opportunity to be in each other's company." Then turning to Sabrina and giving her a knowing glance, he said, "Let me go tell the fellows that I'm out, and I'll meet up with you at the door, a'ight?"

"Okay," Sabrina replied and bit down on her bottom lip like a schoolgirl. "Don't be long either."

"You don't have to worry about that." Tremaine winked while backpedaling in the opposite direction.

"Um, now, what was that about?" Ciara teased, already knowing that her girl was about to get some. Sabrina's girlish smile only gave credibility to what she had already figured out. Holding her hand out, palm up, Ciara said, "All right. What are you waiting for? Put 'em right here."

Dropping the keys in Ciara's hand, Sabrina whined in her thick, Southern drawl, "Girl, please, don't be mad at me. Please." Searching Ciara's eyes for understanding, she said, "I used to be so-o-o in love with him. Tremaine was my first love, girl."

"No way," Ciara said with a mixture of shock and excitement. "Girl, I'm not mad at you. I understand. Enjoy yourself, and be sure to have a little fun for me too." She truly hoped that the remainder of Sabrina's night would be glorious.

"I will, girl. I promise." Leaning forward to hug Ciara, she said, "I'll give you a call tomorrow," before hurriedly heading toward the exit. She drew leering glances due to her nasty, gap-legged stride and thick, brown, slightly bowed legs as she moved through the crowd.

Laughing at the irony of her situation, Ciara found it funny that as horny as she had become due to thoughts of a man she had only shared a fleeting glance with, her girl would more than likely receive the animalistic pounding that she yearned for. At that moment, she concluded that no sooner than she solved the case she had been sent to investigate, she would begin to create a healthy life for herself.

She too needed to love and be loved in return, and the final glance she tossed over her shoulder at the wall-to-wall club patrons as she headed toward the exit was in the hopes that her mysterious dream man would appear before her eyes. But as Ciara made her way to the door, it was obvious that they weren't meant to encounter each other. "Where are you?" were the last words she whispered as she headed out the door.

After virtually exploring the entire club and still coming up short, it slowly began to register that regardless of how hard Dominique searched for the elusive female, he wouldn't find her tonight. So with that realization, he figured that he might as well call it quits and return to the VIP and enjoy the remainder of the festivities along with the rest of his crew.

Heading up the winding staircase to the VIP lounge, his eyes were drawn to the club's exit for some odd reason. Stopping in his tracks, he couldn't believe that she was there. After searching high and low for her, she was actually about to walk out the door.

Without another thought, he did something that, up until this moment, was foreign to him. Unable to understand his actions, he ran down the steps and raced through the club, attempting to catch her. It was a long shot that he would succeed due to the distance and the crowd that stood between them, but nothing would stop him from trying to catch up with the one woman he had to have. He pushed aside people, dodging and weaving between them with unnatural grace. He was moving so quickly that the bystanders had no time to react or protest. Their only response was a bemused gape as he flew by. The entire club seemed to move in slow motion compared to his fervent movements. When he finally arrived outside, there was no sign of her. All he could do was make a vow to himself that the next time, he would not miss.

Chapter 7

Watching her step as she carefully made her way through the open door, Ciara, from the corner of her eye, noticed how the Black, middle-aged bank president glanced down at her ass. The businesslike skirt suit fit tightly over her ample backside, stretching the already formfitting material to accommodate her curvy figure.

"So, other than what you initially told the other agents, this is all you can add to my notes, Mr. . . . ." Peering down at her iPad and notes that were cataloged, she added, ". . . Dean?" in one breath, as if she hadn't actually forgotten.

Instantly averting his eyes from Ciara's behind at the realization that he'd been caught staring, he rapidly blinked, faking as if he had something caught in his eye before stammering. "Um . . . uh . . . Yes, Agent Valentine. I think that I've pretty much told you every-thing I remember."

Dreamily running his eyes over her glorious frame, somewhere within his old, overworked mind, Mr. Dean concluded that if he played his cards right, he might have a chance with the beautiful agent. Thus, although he spoke in his best player impersonation before any sequence of words had begun to leave his mouth, he had already failed. "Is it Ms. Valentine and not Mrs.?" he asked, subtly licking his lips in what he felt was tempting.

Wanting with all her heart and soul to handle the situ-ation in a businesslike manner, the melancholy look that passed between her and Sabrina was more than Ciara could handle. *"Excuse me?"* she questioned, turning beet red. Just the sight of Sabrina virtually doubled over in laughter behind the older, slightly balding gentleman was enough to make her choke as she attempted to control the laughter that threatened to erupt at any second.

"Oh, I was just wondering whether you were married," he stated, oblivious to the tears of mirth pouring from Sabrina's eyes. Had he turned around to see what was happening behind him instead of searching Ciara's finger for a wedding ring, he would have realized what a spectacle he was making of himself.

She followed his eyes to her finger and said, "It's *Agent* Valentine. But I'm happily married, Mr. Dean." Changing the subject in her haste to get away, she announced, "Well, that pretty much wraps up our business here. I appreciate your assistance, and if we need to speak with you further, we'll be in touch."

"Oh, okay," he replied, not quite ready to give up. "If I remember anything else, I'll be sure to call you," he added, raising her business card in the air. In his mind, he felt that there was still a chance for the two of them if he played his cards right.

"Uh-h-h, girl," Sabrina hissed, faking like she was about to be sick.

Frowning at her partner, Ciara released the laughter she had been holding in as she placed the key into the ignition and brought the sports car to life.

"On second thought, the two of you would have made a handsome couple," Sabrina teased with a straight face.

"Yeah, right, bitch. I got your 'handsome couple' right here," Ciara said, flicking her middle finger up in mock anger. Receiving a series of loud, raucous laughter in response to her reply, she had no option but to join in.

Finally, bringing her laughter under control, Ciara decided that Sabrina had some explaining of her own to do. Before today, they hadn't spoken since Friday night. Sabrina had not only reneged on her promise to contact her Saturday, but she had also missed Sunday as well, and Ciara felt that an explanation was in order. Turning to face Sabrina as she navigated the Jaguar through the heavy lunch-hour traffic, she asked, "What happened to you Saturday? I could have sworn you promised to call me. Or maybe you meant Sunday. Oops . . . My bad. You didn't call Sunday either," she said sarcastically.

No longer laughing, Sabrina eyed her intently. As she bit down on her bottom lip, a spark suddenly appeared in her brown eyes, causing her features to illuminate the brightest smile Ciara could ever recall seeing upon her girl's face. "What happened was I was completely swept off my feet for two glorious days. Girl, I can't even begin to tell you the many things that man did to me. Never, and I do mean *never,* have I been pampered and ravished like that nigga, Tremaine, did me." The deep blush covering her face said it all. Shaking her head to clear the memory, Sabrina momentarily looked off at the traffic in a daze.

Just watching her partner's reaction to the weekend she'd spent with her ex was more than enough to let Ciara know that it had truly been mind-boggling. And although she wished nothing less than the best for her girl, deep down inside, due to her own loveless life, jealousy fought its way to the surface. She wanted to be swept off her feet by Prince Charming as well.

"Oh yeah, girl. I almost forgot to tell you," Sabrina said in alarm, jarring Ciara from her thoughts.

"Tell me what?" Placing her eyes on the road and the briskly moving traffic, Ciara loathed the fact that she was jealous of Sabrina's happiness. She had never been jealous, so what she was experiencing was so unlike her.

"Girl, we're invited to a cookout and pool party that Tremaine's throwing at his house this weekend. Wait until you see his house, Ciara. But anyway . . ." she rambled on excitedly. "You *have* to come with me. I promise you that you'll enjoy yourself. Believe me," she declared, smiling at the thought of all the wealthy bachelors that would be present and available for Ciara to select from.

Only, at that moment, thoughts of Dominique invaded Sabrina's mind. And to think that she had never considered introducing the two. He had come to visit Tremaine while she was there this past weekend, and they had caught up on lost time during the visit. As she quickly learned, many things had changed for Dominique, Tremaine, and their whole crew. They were no longer reckless, young, dumb, and full of cum. Each of the old crew had found wealth and prosperity.

"I don't know if I'm going to be able to make it, Sabrina. I need to buckle down and search through all the information we've compiled. I'm sure that somewhere in this maze of reports is the one clue that will lead us to the culprits responsible for the string of robberies," Ciara argued. However, whether or not she knew it, her words had fallen on deaf ears again.

"To hell with the robberies and the robbers. For one day—next Saturday—you and I will be at Tremaine's party. So, unless the robbers are there, we won't be investigating anything." With her lips tightly pressed together in defiance, Sabrina rolled her eyes and neck in the same motion. Since she received no objection from her ghetto gesture, it was pretty much decided by the popping sound Ciara made as she flicked a long strand of hair out of her face and placed her attention back on the road that the party and their presence there was a done deal.

As Sabrina raised the volume on the stereo and turned toward the passenger window to hide her smirk, the devious plan that circulated through her mind slowly began to take form. Now that she had come up with the idea of hooking up Ciara and Dominique, she would settle for nothing less than success.

Chapter 8

Making his daily rounds of Paragon I and II with Sue close on his heels, taking notes, Dominique, as always, felt a sense of pride. Out of his many successful business ventures, the club was his baby. No matter how wealthy he became and what other strides he made, Club Paragon would never be forgotten.

"Hello, Mr. Valiant," a stripper named Strawberry called from across the room. Leaning on the bar with nothing on but a G-string and a pair of stilettos, she created an alluring picture with all her goodies on display. The way she expertly wrapped her thick lips around the banana and swallowed more than ate it made no mystery of what she really wanted to do to her boss.

"Hey, Strawberry," Dominique replied, never slowing his progress. Inwardly smiling at the blatant advance, he couldn't ignore her beauty, but he wouldn't entertain it, either. Regardless of how much the strippers flaunted or advertised free pussy before him, his rule was written in stone: *"Employees first and foremost, so they are off-limits."*

"Hello, Mr. Valiant, my ass," Sue stated in a venomous tone. "Get your ass downstairs somewhere and put on some fuckin' clothes. You know better than running around here like that before the club opens." Shooting daggers at Strawberry, she stood stark still with a no-nonsense look pasted on her face and her hands resting on her Cavalli jean-encased hips.

Giving Sue a stank look as she slowly twirled the banana deeper into her throat for her boss's benefit, Strawberry sucked her teeth and sashayed out of the bar area.

Between the amusement Dominique was receiving from Sue's explosive temper and Strawberry's outright disdain for her, he couldn't decide whether to speak on Sue's angry outburst or continue to watch Strawberry's cinnamon-colored ass cheeks as they jiggled invitingly. However, after blinking to clear his vision, he turned to Sue and asked, "What was that all about? You good?"

"Yeah, I'm fine. I just don't like that arrogant bitch. She's trouble, Dominique, and I'm telling you, I don't like the vibe she's brought to this club."

Smirking, Dominique concluded that although Sue had come to be known as his second in command, and she ran the club with an iron fist, this time, he felt that her attitude was fueled by nothing more than jealousy. Thus, he put very little emphasis or thought into her disdain and mistrust of Strawberry.

"Oh yeah, before I forget, order thirty more cases of Krug Champagne. I don't know what's going on lately, but it seems that ever since the Cristal Corporation announced that they don't want the Black community to embrace their product, sales of Cristal have been down drastically, and we can't keep enough Krug," Dominique said.

"Sure thing, Dominique. I'll get right on it," Sue announced, snapping out of her previous frame of mind. Writing down the last request, she asked, "Okay. Can you think of anything else that needs to be taken care of? Because this list just about covers it, and I pretty much need to get to work. In a couple of hours, this place will be packed." She sighed softly and replaced a long strand of curly hair that fluttered into her eye from the clasp that held the rest of her tresses in place on top of her head.

"No, that pretty much takes care of everything," Dominique said, turning his attention away from the long, lustrous dark curls that framed Sue's face and the remembrance of how he used to wrap them around his hands and drive his length into her tight, molten center. Just the thought alone caused an erection, making him quickly avert his attention from her and the memory of a time and place they could never reenact.

"Well, I gotta go, boss." Waving her hand dismissively, she teased, "Somebody's got to run this joint. So, as usual, it may as well be me."

Briefly watching her walk away with a mischievous smile pasted on her face, Dominique grinned, thinking that he not only possessed the liveliest, most breathtaking club in the city, but he had also been lucky enough to acquire the most prized and sought-after assistant in Atlanta. For that alone, he truly felt as if the gods had blessed him.

As he quickly took the stairs leading to his office with the thought of just how wonderful his life was, Dominique's mind, on its own accord, flashed back to the scene of him chasing the mysterious woman through the club only days before. Not quite sure of how he felt about the whole episode, opening the door to his office, the sight before him instantly erased any other thoughts he may have had on the issue.

"Well, it's about time you decided to grace me with your presence," Tremaine grinned. "I was wondering if you planned to come up here."

Tossing Tremaine a patronizing wink, Dominique used his suede, Gucci-loafered foot to close the door as he made his way across the vast office and removed his friend's gator-booted feet from his plush couch. The couch had cost him a small mint. It was made from

Persian silk and had been purchased during a vacation in the Middle East.

Dropping down in the spot where Tremaine's feet had just lay, he unbuttoned another button on his peach and white starched, striped Burberry shirt and leaned back into the comfort of his prized office possession. "Um . . . That feels good," he announced, slapping Tremaine a pound as he sat upright. "Now, to answer your statement, of course, I was coming up here. This is where I work, you know? Shit, if you did more than dress fly, chase pussy, and floss all damn day, *you* could be at work. Then I'd be in *your* presence." Smirking after his statement, he could only shake his head at the boyish grin that lingered on Tremaine's face.

"Yeah, you do have a point," Tremaine agreed. "But we both know that *I'm* the one that really oversees our dynasty. If I didn't ride around all day 'flossing,' as you say, I wouldn't be able to keep an eye on our vast real estate properties throughout the city. As far as my dressing fly and chasing pussy goes, what's the use in owning a strip mall and three five-star restaurants if you don't frequent them with the best-looking ladies in the city? Hey, and for the record, you're far from a slouch in the flossing, fly dressing, pussy-chasing category your damn self."

Erupting in a fit of laughter, both of them received a jolt of cheer from Tremaine's partially true statement. Their holdings were undoubtedly vast, but the excuses Tremaine used to validate his immature actions were outright outlandish.

"Yo, Dom P," Tremaine began after regaining his composure, "I'm having a cookout at my crib this Saturday. You've got to roll through, man. You already know how I do it. The joint's gonna be off the chain."

"You know what? I think I *will* shoot through." The memory of Tremaine's last party was still fresh in Dominique's mind. He knew his man's announcement of the party being off the chain was merely an under-statement. If anything, by the end of the evening, he was betting that it would more or less spiral into an orgy.

"Shit, now that I think about it, I almost forgot," Tremaine blurted out, slapping the palm of his hand against his forehead. "I met Sabrina's friend the other night in Club Kaya, and believe me when I tell you, she's a sight for sore eyes. Man, you have got to meet—"

Cutting Tremaine off in midsentence, Dominique exhaled and stood up. "Look, I know where this is going, so thanks, but no thanks. Hook up Treon, Pimp, or Money. I'm good."

Watching Dominique stalk off with a look of annoy-ance, Tremaine said, "Well, excuse the hell out of me. I'm sorry for trying to hook you up with the coldest fe-male you've ever had in your damn stable." Smiling at the stubborn look Dominique tossed him after his words, Tremaine had little doubt that his dog heard loud and clear his revelation that she was even badder than any-thing he'd ever had in his stable. Though he realized that not even that would force Dominique to recant his refusal, Tremaine was aware that deep down inside, wanting to hear more about Sabrina's friend was eat-ing up his partner. And although he wouldn't reveal the knowledge to Dominique, she had already been invited to the party, so he would get the chance to meet her in the flesh, regardless of whether he wanted to.

Chapter 9

Cruising through the exclusive Alpharetta subdivision, Ciara, riding shotgun in the Jaguar's passenger seat while Sabrina navigated the sports car, was in awe as she viewed each of the vast estates that were safely situated behind tall, gated structures. Amazed at the indescribable, spectacular homes looming ahead of her, if not for the designer Michael Kors shades that covered her eyes, the bubbling of excitement she was experiencing would have easily been evident by her big, bulging gray orbs.

"Ooh, there it is, Ciara. That's Tremaine's house up ahead," Sabrina pointed excitedly.

"Up where?" Ciara asked. Staring in the direction that Sabrina's finger pointed, she raised her shades to make sure that she was seeing what she thought she was seeing. "That . . . that . . . is his house . . . right there?" she stuttered in disbelief.

"Yep, it sure is," Sabrina proudly announced. "I told you he was living the life of the rich and famous."

Pulling up to the tall security gate and passing their invitation to one of the white-jacketed, dark shade-wearing men, they were promptly ushered up the long, winding, circular driveway. A valet instantly approached the car and graciously opened the doors for them to exit before commandeering their vehicle and parking it in the large, grassy area that held forty or more luxury vehicles that easily dwarfed their own in comparison.

Openly staring but trying with all she possessed not to, the numerous Benzes, Ranges, Porsches, and trucks of every make and model garnered her undivided attention. But the metallic Bentley GT she eyed as she followed Sabrina up the white marble walkway nearly caused her to stumble. Straightening up before anyone noticed her slight indiscretion, Ciara quickly glanced down at her Via Spiga pumps to ensure they were still intact, then sped up to catch her girl. She found herself wondering what Tremaine did for a living.

Reaching the rear of the house where the festivities were in full swing, Ciara abruptly halted her steps. Peering at her girl to see if the scene had made her uncomfortable as well, unlike herself, Sabrina was grooving to the loud music as if she were truly in her element. *How is this possible?* Ciara was truly stumped.

As she beheld the scene that transpired before her, it was instantly apparent that she was overdressed in her satin Gucci Capri's and matching halter top. For the most part, the rest of the women wore the skimpiest bikinis they could find. Many were in various stages of undress, and if Ciara's eyes weren't playing tricks on her, she could have sworn that off in the distance, two women were intertwined in a naked embrace.

"Uh . . . um . . . Sabrina, This isn't my type of party," Ciara declared, balling her face up at the sight of a bejeweled man laughing loudly as he chased a half-naked female around the pool while pouring champagne over her head, eliciting giggles and laughs from her and their audience. Just as she turned to leave, she felt a firm but gentle hand grasp her shoulder and pull her into a friendly embrace.

"Hello, ladies. I see you've finally arrived," Tremaine said in his soothing but matter-of-fact tone as he reached out and hugged a smiling Sabrina with his other arm.

With a delighted glint in his bright green eyes, he grinned at Ciara and added, "I see you've also had your first glimpse of Treon." He peered off in the distance at Treon as he caught up with the squealing woman and tossed her into the pool.

"Oh, girl, he's harmless. That's just my homie, Treon. I'll introduce you to the whole gang before we leave," Sabrina said, dismissing Ciara's objections as she snuggled up closer to Tremaine.

"Yeah, I can't wait to meet the gang," Ciara replied in a tone that dripped with sarcasm. However, it was apparently missed because Sabrina grabbed Tremaine's hand and began leading him toward the enormous house.

Tremaine reached for Ciara's hand and said, "Come on, young lady. Let me give you a tour of my humble abode."

Instantly twisting her face up in a manner that said, *"Please,"* Ciara said, "I'd love to take a tour of your home, but for the record, the last thing this house could ever be called is a 'humble abode.'"

"Girl, come on here." Tremaine smiled, leading the two women up to the house.

"Tremaine, your home is absolutely breathtaking, and I thank you for inviting me to your little . . . I mean, big gathering," Ciara corrected, gazing around the huge yard at what looked to be hundreds of partygoers.

"Thanks for the compliment on the house, but party or no party, you're always welcome to visit. Any friend of Sabrina's is automatically my people as well." Pouring another round of champagne and orange juice for the women and Rémy VSOP for himself, he glanced down at his diamond-encrusted Jacob watch with a white, crocodile band to match his Armani slacks and matching short-sleeved Izod button-down. "Would you ladies please excuse me?" he said, winking his eye conspiratorially at Sabrina as he removed a miniature platinum-colored phone from his Dolce & Gabbana belt and walked off to make a quick call.

Glancing down at her watch as she sipped the delicious mimosa concoction that Tremaine had introduced her to, Ciara decided she had experienced enough fun for one day. The crowd was thickening, and as the sun slowly began to set, it was starting to seem as if the saying, "The freaks come out at night," had some validity to it because the women who had been partially nude earlier, for the most part, were next to naked now. And to make matters worse, in the Jacuzzi, two grotesquely muscular Black men had a pretty, petite, white woman's breasts stuck in each of their mouths.

Turning up the remainder of her drink, Ciara turned toward Sabrina, who was grooving in her seat to Sean Paul and Keyshia Cole's "Give It Up To Me," and announced, "I came, I drank, and I ate enough barbecue to hold me for a lifetime. And after meeting and having to fight off all your crazy-ass homeboys, I'm ready to go."

"Ciara, no, you can't leave yet." Realizing that she may have slipped, she said, "I . . . um . . . I mean, we can't leave yet." Averting eye contact with her friend, she looked into the crowd hoping to spot Dominique.

"No, that's where you're wrong, my friend. You may be staying, but I, on the other hand, am about to be out." Placing her glass on the table as she stood and smoothed her tight pants in place, making sure that her attire was flawless, she added, "By the lusty looks that have been passing between the two of you for the last few hours, it's fair to assume that you're staying. Am I correct?"

"I just got off the phone with Dominique, and he's on his way," Tremaine announced. "He'll be pleased to meet you, for sure, Ciara." Receiving a frown from Sabrina, he was just about to ask what was wrong when Ciara answered his question.

"Well, I'd be pleased to meet him as well, but just not today. Thanks for a wonderful evening, but I must call it a night since I have a party pooper reputation to uphold."

"Have one more drink with us before you run off. It's still early, Ciara." Then reaching for the champagne, Tremaine hoped his persuasive skills would work right now, if at no other time.

Momentarily pausing at the mention of the time and another exotic drink, Ciara thought better of the invitation and graciously declined. Saying her goodbyes one last time, she promptly made her exit.

Once the valet had retrieved the Jaguar and the convertible top had been raised to suit her needs, Ciara placed a Mary J. Blige CD in the stereo and departed the long driveway. However, her jaw nearly dropped into her lap at her first, up close and personal sight of an actual Rolls-Royce Phantom. The two automobiles passed with so little distance between them that she could have reached through her window and smeared the baby-blue mirrored paint job that looked like it had been sprayed with wax only seconds ago. Though she was only privy to the sight of the driver's short, curly hair due to his seeming to be searching for something in the console area, his dark complexion only served to compliment the snow-white interior. Yet, what Ciara saw as the icing on the cake was the gold that adorned every fixture on the Rolls-Royce that should have been silver.

Reaching the end of the driveway and having to remove her eyes from the most beautiful car she had ever seen and marveling at the rarity of riding in one, much less owning it, the words continued to reverberate in her head, *Who the hell is the driver of my dream on wheels?*

Chapter 10

"There you go," Dominique said to himself, finally recovering his cell phone after having to fish it from beneath the passenger seat. Placing his attention back on the long driveway that led up to Tremaine's mansion, the reflection of a Jaguar that he couldn't recall passing lingered in his side mirror before heading through the gate and out of his view. Deciding that he was just glad they hadn't collided, he let the thought slip from his mind as he pulled in front of the mansion and exited the car looking and feeling like a true don.

"How are you this evening, Mr. Valiant?" the valet asked, admiring Dominique's diamond-flooded chain. It was evident by the way that his eyes bulged out that he had never seen the likes of such an excessive piece of jewelry as what hung around his boss's neck.

Inwardly smiling, Dominique tossed the youngster his keys and said, "I'm doing just fine. Be sure to take care of my baby, a'ight, Jason?" Noting how the young man's head snapped in his direction at the realization that his boss had actually called him by name, Dominique winked knowingly. Like most of the other people hired for this party, Jason was recruited from other clubs that Dominique owned.

Little did Jason know, it had become a point for Dominique to know every one of his employees' names long ago. The good thing was, at times like this, just seeing the excitement that emanated from someone when they were addressed by name made the time and practice he had undertaken to accomplish such a feat worthwhile.

"What's up, boy? You finally made it with your late ass!" Money slurred loudly, drawing attention to Dominique's arrival.

"Dom P, what's good, nigga?" Treon, the official life of every party, carried a big bottle of Cognac. His lowered eyelids and the stagger in his steps showed that he had been drinking heavily from it.

Extending complimentary pounds to each of his partners, Dominique removed a large Cuban cigar from his lavender Gucci button-down pocket. Snipping the tip and using the gold lighter he retrieved from his thin, white Gucci slacks, he allowed a wisp of smoke to curl upward from his slightly parted lips before announcing, "We need to gather the others for an emergency meeting." Noticing just how quickly their demeanors changed from fun to business in seconds, he couldn't help the instant admiration that surfaced for two of the four closest and most loyal friends a man could ever have.

Moving with lightning speed, Money informed, "I'll go round up the others."

Treon said, "Let me excuse myself from my fan club over there."

Following his man's eyes to a group of top-dollar strippers, Dominique took another hit of his cigar and nodded to the women who had caught sight of him and were waving excitedly.

As he watched his partners heading off to handle their respective business, he removed a glass of champagne from one of the silver trays carried by a legion of waiters and noticed the stunning women who paraded around the grounds. An array of beauties who worked at Paragon were there, but true to form, they were putting in overtime with the many sports players lounging by the pool and Jacuzzi flaunting their wealth. Much platinum, gold, and diamonds were in view, worn by Atlanta Hawks, Falcons, and Braves players who had no problem paying like they weighed.

On the flip side, some of the city's most talented gold diggers were on their hands, knees, and backs to put their bids in. In addition, the baddest, freakiest strippers from Paragon, Jazzy T's, Body Tap, Gentlemen's Club, Blue Flame, Pleasures, and Strokers were on hand to do whatever was necessary to relieve the players and some of ATL's biggest ballers of their money.

Ready to get the meeting over and return to the festivities that would surely intensify once darkness fell, Dominique headed toward the house and office inside, where he knew his crew would be waiting.

Rejoining the party and mixing with the guests as he made his rounds, Dominique had all but forgotten his earlier wish to meet with his crew. They had quickly handled their business. With everything back on point, he too was content and enjoying the show. And without a doubt, a show of some sort was taking place in every shadow.

Comfortable, Ciara leaned against the large pillows she had propped up against the headboard hours ago. After showering, she changed into her pajamas and got in bed. It was after 2:00 a.m., and she was engrossed in investigative reports, surveillance photos from numerous banks, and witness statements. What caught her as odd was that the suspects had all but cleaned out every vault within three minutes in each robbery.

Ciara couldn't shake the gut feeling that pulling off something of such great magnitude was impossible without an inside link. Someone had to be filtering them the information, but who? And how would she possibly find out? She had no idea, but as she dropped her pen down on the pad she'd been taking notes on, exhaled, and removed her reading glasses, she decided she had done all she could for one night. There would be no easy way to solve this one, and she would be fooling herself if she thought the answers would tumble out of thin air.

At least for this case, she would use the patience that the instructors at the Academy had attempted to drill into her at every possible chance. They had taught that patience was the key to victory. The Bureau's statistics surely proved that by leaps and bounds. It was not just shown to be accurate, but their motto was that every criminal who got away with something continued to commit crimes. Therefore, it was only a matter of time before the bank robbers made a mistake. A mistake was what Ciara was counting on, and if statistics were to be relied on, then the men she sought would make one before it was all over. Smiling at the thought, she planned to be there when they did.

Chapter 11

The black Yukon holding the five robbers parked in the fire lane, directly in front of the downtown bank. It drew a few questioning stares from some pedestrians who scurried past on their preplanned paths. Yet, there was nothing unusual or abnormal about a group of well-dressed men sitting in an expensive vehicle on Peachtree Street. This knowledge emboldened the bank robbers' crew to forego precautions and play their objective closer than they would have at the beginning of their careers. They had done this more times than they could recall and, like anything else, practice more or less created perfection.

"There's our mark," the leader announced, eyeing the armored car carrying their awaited shipment. Then glancing down at his trusted diver's watch, he stated, "They may be late, but like clockwork, they're here with our money."

Chuckles ensued from the four others peering at the heavily armored car that suddenly came to a halt up ahead. Though they laughed at their leader's proclamation, like him, they too had already taken the liberty of claiming the money as their own as well.

Calmly watching as the unloading process took place, it was funny to them that the guards who wielded an array of weaponry while protecting the large pallet of money on its way into the bank would leave as soon as the money was safely inside. With their exit, the money would be ripe for the taking. Who could stop them? It surely wouldn't be possible for the aging security guard to do it.

"Okay, here we go." No sooner than the words were out of his mouth, the leader lowered his tinted Ray-Ban shades over his eyes and pulled the soft leather gloves over his big hands. Then placing the extended clip into the fully automatic M1 that hung over his shoulder beneath his designer sports coat, he watched his partners duplicating his actions and observed the guards closing the door to their vehicle and pulling off.

"What are we waiting for? Let's get this shit over with and get the hell out of Dodge," one of the crewmen exclaimed. Putting his earpiece in as he looked around the vehicle and received exhilarated looks, no other words were necessary as four eager men piled out of the truck. This was the moment that they each yearned for. And although it had never really been spoken, even more than the money they had compiled from the robberies, the power surge they experienced from each one was what spurred them on.

"Everyone, drop! And I mean right now." The order was given in a loud, no-nonsense voice that left no doubt in the minds of the bank's patrons. If anyone had thought about disobeying the order before, the sight of the security guard lying unconscious in a puddle of his own blood quickly relinquished any further foolish thoughts.

Taking his place on the counter where he had an unobstructed view of the bank and the people cowering on the floor, the robber who had given the order to get down waved his weapon and yelled, "Place your hands on top of your heads! And I'd better not catch any of you eyeballing me or my people." Then nodding to his crew, who had removed large tote bags as they headed toward the rear of the bank, he hit the three-minute timer on his watch and said, "Phase one is clear."

Hearing him clearly through their earpieces, the leader and two of his crew moved quickly toward the desk of the person they thought should have been near. "Get your ass up," the leader blared, finding the bank manager lying face down beneath his desk.

"Sir, please . . . Please, don't hurt me," the manager pleaded tearfully.

They didn't have time for this, and he didn't plan to repeat himself. Reaching down to grab a handful of the manager's tie, he yanked the fearful, older, balding white man up from the floor. Choking him in the process without worrying about the man's health, the leader ignored the man's strangled breaths and pulled him through the steel door and gates on the other side.

Moving through the glistening hallway at breakneck speed, they were each alerted by their partner, who stood guard over the bank's patrons, that they had two minutes and thirty seconds remaining. However, as soon as the announcement had cleared their earpieces, they turned to the left and came into contact with the door they sought at the end of the corridor.

Pushing the manager in front of them, the leader gave him a piercing stare, and with a death grip on his throat, he hissed, "You only have one opportunity to open this door, so I suggest that you punch the right numbers into that keypad. And just in case you have any smart ideas, know it's up to you whether you live or die in the next few moments."

Taking only a millisecond to decide after viewing the scary weapons and expressions in the eyes of his captors, the manager quickly began to punch in the code that would allow entrance into the vault. As he shot nervous glances at the robbers, his palms were sweating profusely, and the only thought in his mind was making it home safely.

However, when the sound of the vault opening was heard, the manager's thoughts abruptly ended as he crumbled to the floor with the force of a heavy sack of potatoes. He would live to make it home as he had hoped, but thanks to the pressure of the M1 that crashed into the base of his skull, he would never forget the white men who had caused his massive headache when he awoke.

"A'ight, let's pack up our money and get the hell out of here," the leader said, stepping over the unconscious manager on his way into the vault. Eyeing the pallet of money that sat in the middle of the floor surrounded by wall-to-wall safety deposit boxes, pride and appreciation were evident in his smile.

He promptly unzipped his bag and followed suit with the two members of his crew who were packing the huge bundles of banded bills. Their adrenaline was raging. The few million they hurriedly packed was enough to make any man's adrenaline do the same. But the men in the vault weren't just any men. These men were elite. And now, thanks to the on-point information they had received once again, this would be calculated as the four-teenth successful hit for the rich and seemingly famous robbers. Thus, in their mind, the world was theirs.

Chapter 12

"Yeah," Ciara said into the receiver. The smile she had previously worn before the call was now a thing of the past. "Uh-huh." She exhaled subconsciously and slumped her shoulders in the seat.

"What?" Sabrina mumbled the question, tearing her eyes from the road and attempting to discover what had occurred to change her partner's demeanor.

Ciara waved her off, pointing her finger aggressively toward the traffic as she continued speaking into the receiver pinned between her face and shoulder. She rummaged through her purse and pulled out her iPad in her rush to record the data she received. "A'ight. Where did you say this took place . . .? Right. I'm aware of that . . ." she frowned and lowered her eyes angrily. ". . . Yes, I understand. We'll be there as soon as we . . . *Bitch!*" she blurted out and tossed the dead phone to the floorboard.

"Damn, what was that about?" Sabrina questioned, noticing the apparent anger from her friend.

"Our suspects have struck again. They hit a bank downtown not even an hour ago. And to make matters worse, that panther-looking bitch you work for just hung up on me. Ughhh . . . I would love to kick her ugly ass."

Snickering, Sabrina tried to keep a straight face when Ciara cut her eyes evilly in her direction. "A'ight, a'ight. I'm sorry." She swallowed, making a funny face that also brought a chuckle from Ciara. "So, I take it that she wants to see us, right?"

Nodding her head, Ciara answered Sabrina's next question before it was asked. "The bank is on Peachtree Street, and in case you didn't already know, that's where you and I are headed before we return to headquarters." Watching Sabrina shaking her head, like her partner, she too was disgusted with the new turn of events for the day.

Strolling through the crime scene with the bank manager and Sabrina close on her heels, Ciara tried her best to play out the robbery as it had been given to her by the manager, security guard, and numerous customers.

"Do you need medical attention before we continue?" Ciara couldn't help worrying about the manager. With each step he took, it seemed as though he winced in pain, and she could recall the nasty lump that sat at the base of his skull when they met.

"No, I'm . . . I'm fine," he replied, mustering more confidence than his squinting eyes evidenced. "I can get this little lump taken care of later. Right now, I want to help you catch and convict the men who did this." He smiled weakly and said, "Follow me so I can show you how they came straight to my desk and got me. Somehow, they knew exactly who I was."

Finding it odd that they had known who the manager was without having to question any of the employees, Ciara's attention was suddenly riveted to a young Black female being interviewed nearby.

". . . I'm telling you, man. Those were four of the coolest white men I've ever seen in my 23 years on earth." Then rolling her neck to emphasize the point she was trying to make, she added, "On second thought, I don't care how white they looked, them muthafuckas are from the hood."

Recognizing how serious and passionate a tone the young female had responded in, Ciara found herself drawn to the interview. Then quickly cutting the manager's rambling short, she turned to Sabrina.

"Look, I need you to deal with him." She nodded toward the bank manager. "I heard something, and I'd like to investigate it."

"I got it under wraps. Go ahead."

Excusing herself, Ciara quickly returned to the detective and the young lady who stood nearby. The female's stance was arrogant and unbending. With her hands on her hips and a scowl on her pretty brown face, she presented a picture that defined her belief in whatever she had been trying to explain to the detective.

Removing her FBI credentials, Ciara flashed them to the detective and announced, "I'll take over from here." His relief was evident because he failed to put up the slightest argument as he turned and stalked off.

"Damn. I like how you just rolled up and pulled rank on that clown. I don't be feeling Atlanta police no how." The woman sucked her teeth in protest and smiled, showing a mouthful of pearly white, evenly spaced teeth.

Returning the smile and extending her hand, Ciara said, "I'm Agent Valentine. And you are?"

"My name is Marcia." Then shaking Ciara's hand, she said, "I hope that this doesn't take long 'cause I've got to pick up my son from day care, and I'm already running late."

Nodding her head in understanding, Ciara said, "I promise you, this will only take a few more minutes. What brought me over here was your opinion that the robbers were somehow from the hood. Could you explain what would make you think that?"

"Okay. It's about time that someone wants to listen to what I've got to say," she said excitedly. "I'm just gonna keep it real. They walked through this joint like they were up in the club, flossing and shit."

Taking in the words she just heard, Ciara's mind was flipping through the numerous possibilities that Marcia's statement had opened up to her. For some reason that she couldn't quite figure out herself, she couldn't wait to see the surveillance tapes. With this new information at her disposal, she was sure to see the tapes in a whole new light.

Ciara was deep in thought as she sat in Sabrina's luxuriously furnished condominium. This had been their mode of operation when work hours officially ended each day since the last robbery had been carried out three days before. So, as they watched the bank's surveillance tapes again for the tenth consecutive time and compared it to the tapes from the previous robberies, Ciara's mind was transported back to the day of the robbery and the meeting they were summoned to after leaving the bank . . .

The head agent's office needed a paint job. As Ciara glanced at the dullness of the interior, she concluded that some brighter furniture, a few pictures on the wall, and a couple of plants placed strategically throughout the room couldn't hurt.

"Boom!"

The door slammed and caught Sabrina and Ciara off guard. The young agents turned and came face-to-face with Sabrina's boss and Ciara's archrival. Preparing to stand, they each stopped in their tracks upon hearing the agent's statement.

"Don't bother standing. You've both been sitting on your asses for the last couple of weeks, so why expend the unnecessary energy now?" Then making the sharp remark, she held Ciara with a piercing glare and leaned against her desk with folded arms. "Well, which of you is going to give me the load of bullshit I'm sure is coming?"

Noticing the nervous look Sabrina shot her before diverting her eyes to the dingy carpet, Ciara thought that it was a damn shame that her loudmouthed partner was a fuckin' coward. With no other option, she cleared her throat and jumped straight from the pan into the fire.

"Agent Craddock . . . You ugly-ass, panther-looking bitch" is what she wanted to say. "Um . . . We have both worked as hard as possible to catch these men, but—" is what came out instead.

"But nothing," Craddock snapped in a vile tone, standing over Ciara with fire in her eyes. "I'm not trying to hear any excuses. What I want are results. They sent you down here from Washington like you were supposed to be the best or something. But now that you're here, you haven't shown me shit. In fact, our problem has only gotten worse since our robbers got away with another $3,381,069 today." Gnashing her teeth, the agent tossed Ciara a condescending smirk and said, "You sure did turn out to be a flop."

"Let me tell you something, you rotten-toothed, raggedy-ass white bitch!" Ciara moved with lightning speed, sending Agent Craddock shuffling backward, attempting to place the large wooden desk between them. Ciara had heard enough; her outburst was no more than the calm before the storm.

"Ciara!" Sabrina snapped, grabbing hold of her girl's shoulder.

Angry tears clouded her eyes as she glared at the suddenly scared agent shrinking behind the desk. Ciara had reached a boiling point. Had it not been for Sabrina's presence in the room, she did not doubt that her nemesis would have received a well overdue ass whipping.

"Breathe, girl. Come on, now. It's not worth it," Sabrina declared in a soothing voice.

Holding her prey with an unblinking stare, Ciara fol-lowed Sabrina's advice and slowly began to backpedal. However, before exiting the office, she spoke in a voice that cracked with rage and resentment. "For future reference, it might be to your benefit to watch what you say out of that stupid-ass mouth of yours. You wouldn't want to write a check with your mouth that your ass can't cash . . ."

The insistent sound of knocking interrupted Ciara's silent reminiscing. Turning to the door and Sabrina as she hurriedly made her way across the plush white carpet to answer it, Ciara realized that their work might end for the night.

Chapter 13

Dominique whipped through traffic and handled the McLaren SLR Benz with the skill of a trained racecar driver. Out of his small fleet of vehicles, this was the one he enjoyed the most. It was well worth the mid-six-figure fee it had set him back, and the real bonus was that except for a white billionaire he had come into contact with from Miami, no one else in Atlanta drove one.

Exiting the highway and accelerating in his haste to reach Peachtree Street, Dominique peered at the diamond-studded Baume & Mercier that sported a cream crocodile band that matched his shoes. Not surprisingly, he also noticed that, as usual, he was running late. But due to the breakneck speed he had been traveling, as soon as he looked up from his watch, the meeting spot, Justin's, loomed ahead of him.

After parking and speaking to a few associates on his way through the crowded restaurant, he searched the prime tables. He examined everyone seated at them until his eyes locked upon another pair of eyes that were glued to him. Promptly covering the distance between them, his dinner date stood and embraced him in a familiar fashion.

"You look very handsome this evening." Returning to her seat and placing the linen napkin back across her lap, she added, "I already took the liberty of ordering your food and a chilled bottle of Chardonnay for us. Of course, you still eat prime rib, potato salad, buttered string beans, and biscuits, don't you?" The smug grin covering her beautiful face testified that she was confident she had him down to a science.

Dominique nodded, and his smile was response enough. As usual, his longtime friend and dinner guest had not only decided what he needed but also made sure that everything he required was available to him. Some things never changed, and as he watched her pour their drinks, their first meeting a decade earlier materialized in his memory . . .

Hungry, Dominique stood outside the exclusive restaurant and watched from the shadows as richly attired diners came and went. The furred and suited couples who exited in expensive imports, wearing sparkling jewels and even brighter smiles, seemed not to have a care in the world. Yet, Dominique's gnawing insides spoke of the long line of problems he had encountered since arriving in the city.

Exiting the Greyhound months before with grand dreams and his life savings of a few hundred hard-earned dollars, Dominique recalled the bright-eyed demeanor he'd carried like his own personal armor. However, within hours, his bright eyes had become black eyes. Thanks to a group of young men he had unluckily encountered while taking a shortcut through a dark alley, his small suitcase and life savings had been stripped from him. He had quickly found himself in dire straits with no money, clothes, or family to call upon and many cuts and bruises to go along with his black eyes and swollen lips.

Feeling his stomach grumble at the thought of the long wait until the morning, and when the YMCA began to serve breakfast, he took even breaths to still his nerves for the task ahead. He had never committed a crime before, except for stealing candy as a child. Yet, it had come down to survival of the fittest, and at six foot three and 215 pounds, he figured that it was about time that he did what was necessary to eat.

Quickly walking as he exited the shadows where he had been lurking, the man Dominique sought departed the restaurant. Nervous at the prospect of actually robbing someone but intent on doing so, his fists involuntarily clenched and released in anticipation. Raw adrenaline navigated his movements with only a matter of feet separating him from the richly dressed victim. However, with no more than a foot between them, as he raised his arm to strike, from out of thin air, a beautiful female grabbed him and whisked him in the opposite direction.

"Well, it's about time you arrived," she stated to the dismayed male as she held his arm with a viselike grip, ignoring the eyes that followed them.

"Huh?" Dominique mumbled, looking down on the pretty older female. Who is she? And where the hell does she think she's taking me?

She giggled when she deactivated her car alarm and hit the automatic start button on her key ring. "Okay. Either you're crazy, you have a death wish, or you're not from Atlanta. Which one is it?" she questioned, leading him to the passenger side of the new 7 Series BMW.

Dominique's response was a questioning stare.

"Well, since you seem not to know what the hell is going on, how about I explain it to you in the car? Get in," she said, opening the door and walking around to the other side.

Thinking the entire situation was strange, he concluded he had nothing to lose by getting in the car. The way he looked at it, if all else failed, he outweighed her by at least eighty pounds, and she was too gorgeous to have been a threat.

"Now, just so you know, the man you were about to accost is not only our chief of police, but he's also said to be in the Mafia." Instantly witnessing a sick look on his face, she wanted to laugh. It was at that moment that she recognized how handsome he was. Not bad at all, she thought, noticing his dark, muscular frame and short, dark curls. Inwardly smiling, she quickly decided that with a little time and effort, she could do wonders with him.

At that moment, as the expensive BMW headed out into traffic, an unusual and lucrative relationship was formed between the young, homeless man and the theater owner and wife of one of the most respected men in Atlanta . . .

"Dominique, is everything all right, dear? You seem somewhat preoccupied," she said, running her manicured index finger around her glass before sipping her drink.

"No, I'm fine. I was just thinking about how we met and how far I've come in life thanks to you." After tasting his drink, he said, "I owe you a lot, Olivia."

"That you do, darling," she teased, winking her eye.

"Here are your entrées," the waiter announced, placing the numerous dishes on the table and leaving as quickly as he had appeared.

"M-m-m. The food looks delicious. Dig in so we can finish and hurry to my favorite course . . . dessert." She licked her lips.

Dominique smiled, knowing that dessert would indeed be her favorite part of the meal. But in all truth, he too couldn't wait either.

***

"Ah-h-h, *s-s-s-s* . . ." Olivia moaned loudly as she worked her tight, spasming pussy down over Dominique's protruding length.

"That's right. Pop that pussy the way I like it," Dominique commanded, smacking her jiggling red ass. He knew how turned on she got when he talked dirty to her. But as she increased her erratic movements and whimpered as she worked her muscles, he too felt his toes begin to curl while watching her cheeks shimmy and shake.

"Dominique . . . Oh shit. Oh . . . my . . . God," she yelled out, stretching out to grasp his ankles as she rode him even faster.

Raising his hips to meet her stroke for stroke, Dominique stared through wide eyes at the sight of his huge, glistening dick as it appeared and disappeared entirely into her hairy, greedily grasping pussy. It never ceased to amaze him how something as monstrous as his foot-long dick could force itself into a space as tight as Olivia's pussy. However, her loud screams and the following words wiped out any other thoughts besides pleasing her from his mind.

"Oh . . . oh . . . I'm coming. Baby . . . mama's coming. Work it . . . Work it!" she pleaded in a demented voice.

Feeling her juices flowing around his dick, he bit down on his bottom lip, caressed her thick, silky thighs, grabbed her shapely hips, and began to fuck her hard and fast. Ignoring her painful yelps and whimpers, he fucked her roughly, just how he knew she liked it.

Olivia cried out one last time before her orgasm exploded, causing her to go limp as a kaleidoscope of colors burst behind her tightly closed eyes. Unable to control the trembling of her limbs, she groaned with the force of Dominique's eruption. His juices jettisoned against her walls multiple times before he cupped her ass and pulled her down on his rigid dick.

Quiet except for their shallow breathing, neither Olivia nor Dominique stirred. They had been going at it nonstop for hours, and although this had been their ritual for the last ten years, they never seemed to get enough.

"Baby, that was great," Olivia said breathlessly.

"Uh-huh" was Dominique's only reply as he gently stroked her ass. His thoughts were somewhere else.

"What is it? What's wrong?" Rising and allowing his dick to plop out with a loud, sucking sound, Olivia crawled to the head of the bed and lay beside him. She ran her fingers through his soft, damp curls as she patiently awaited his response.

"It's nothing, really. I was only reflecting on our little 'relationship' of sorts." Laughing at the irony of the situation, he announced, "You bought me my first suit, gave me a job in the theater, rented my first apartment, gave me a car, taught me the art of loving a woman, and put me on the road to achieving unbridled riches. Yet, you've never asked for anything in return in all these years."

"Nope, that's where you're wrong. You give me the greatest sex I've ever experienced, and every time I see you, I feel pride that you would never understand." Then grinning, she added, "And don't forget the money you have placed in my account for the last few years. And speaking of money, did you make the deposit?" She asked the question with a raised brow.

"Of course I did. I oversaw the wire transfer to your offshore account myself. So, as of a few hours ago, you're now a quarter of a million dollars richer."

"Good." Her smile magnified as her fingers gently squeezed his dick. Nothing made her hornier than Dominique and a steady, growing bank account. The mention of being $250,000 richer while holding a foot-long at the same time had her juices slowly flowing down her thighs.

Olivia's fingers had easily worked Dominique back to full staff. As she inched her body back down his torso and wrapped her lips around his erection, tired or not, he would never bow out of the competition. So, exhaling as he attempted to catch his third breath, he planned to give her body exactly what it deserved . . . and then some. However, when she abruptly raised her head and peered at him with saliva-drenched lips, his erection partially deflated with her next words.

Holding him with an intense stare, she whispered, "All good things come to those who wait, and since you now have everything you could ever want, cut your losses and get out before it's too late. I've never led you astray, so don't just 'hear' me. Take heed to what I say."

Forcefully pushing her head back down to the task she had begun, he didn't do it so much because he wanted oral stimulation. Dominique figured that he would be spared her advice and ideologies if she were busy. In fact, as he looked down at her through blank eyes, he was glad to see that she wouldn't be able to talk with her mouth full.

Chapter 14

Busily working at his hobby, mixing the precise amounts of chemicals and synthetic plastics, then using the most technologically advanced sprayers to saturate the substance he chose to work on evenly, Dominique was in a peaceful place as he slowly watched his creation come to life. Though this was his hideaway of sorts—the place where he chose to go when he needed time for self—he had never forgotten when or where the interest in the craft had been born in him.

Like so many more of his newfound tastes, Olivia had introduced him to the art. Though she couldn't have had the slightest idea of what her job offer would mean to the young man who she met and virtually saved from self-destruction, the job and appointed position he received at the theater would, in time, reshape his entire existence.

Grinning at the thought of his somewhat unusual past, he had to agree that he had elevated drastically from the measly apprentice of the theater's makeup artist to a multimillionaire entrepreneur. And to think that he had once been in awe of the man's skills, when now, over ten years later, his advanced methods and the ever-growing technology that easily surpassed the old ways of doing things made him a master of creating illusions.

Lifting the intricate mask, the smile on his face broadened tremendously. The average man would have been smiling due to the million-plus that would soon be overflowing in his coffers. Yet, being far from average and already richer than he could have ever dreamed, his happiness resulted from his newest creation. Even more than any mask, what he held in his hands was the true definition of the many faces he wore. Therefore, the aura of mystery he possessed made him happier than any amount of money ever could.

Chapter 15

"Pass the rock, nigga," Treon yelled beneath the basket. "I got this, lame," he insisted, breathing hard with sweat drenching his bare torso.

"Yeah, you got me all right, chump," Tremaine declared, stepping in front of Treon as Pimp passed the ball. Then snatching the pass out of the air that had been meant for Treon, Tremaine faked left. But when Treon took the bait, he flicked the ball backward to Money, who dunked it with two hands and smacked the backboard afterward. "Game, nigga. Now, who's the lame?" Tremaine shouted, giving Money a pound as he smiled victoriously and shoulder leaned tauntingly toward the losers.

"Fuck you, and fuck you too," Treon responded in a defeated tone.

Smiling at his partner and teammate, Pimp couldn't care less whether they had won. He needed something to drink at that moment, so saying, "Good game," as he headed toward the sidelines, he grabbed a towel, wiped the sweat from his brow, and reached for the cooler of water.

"A'ight, why you clowns holding the rock up? Let's ball. I ain't come out here for nothing."

Turning to the approaching voice, Tremaine, Treon, Money, and Pimp each eyed one another with looks that said, *"This nigga can't be serious."* Then shaking their heads, they ignored the intruder and followed Pimp to the sidelines.

"What?" Dominique questioned with an amused look on his face.

"Man, you can't be serious, right? We've been out here ballin' for hours, and now, *as usual,* here you come, looking like a model for Team Jordan, all late and shit." Treon tossed the ball to Dominique, laughed, and said, "There you go, nigga. Enjoy yourself."

After showering and changing their sweaty, ballin' gear, the group gathered in Treon's entertainment room for drinks and their own brand of friendly conversation. Also, there was no lack of things to do with an array of video games, a mini-movie screen, a poker table, a billiard table, and a state-of-the-art stereo system. However, the laughter that loudly rang out in the cavernous room had nothing to do with any of the expensive toys that lined the room. Instead, the merriment was brought about by the comments directed at Dominique. So, although he too shared in the laughter, it was evident that his crew had placed him in the hot seat.

Foolishly glaring at his man from his perch on the edge of the billiard table, Tremaine said, "The nigga had the nerve to have an attitude when I tried to hook him up with Ciara." Then pausing, he spoke in a voice meant to imitate Dominique's. "I'm not interested, Tremaine. Damn. Why don't you just hook her up with Treon, Pimp, or Money?"

"Hell yeah. Why didn't you send her my way?" Pimp exclaimed.

"Nah, I'll gladly take her. You ain't know?" Money blurted out.

"Oh, hell nah," Treon loudly cut in. "That pretty muthafucka ain't got to take her. Shawty's fine ass can easily join my harem. In fact, let a nigga cop her digits from Sabrina next time you holla at her."

Listening closely to their clowning and realizing that their words were all in jest, Dominique couldn't help but read between the lines. His men were each chick magnets, and they didn't just mess with *any* females, either. They had the baddest women in the city fighting for a spot on their team. For them to have been speaking so highly of Sabrina's girl, she had to be exceptional. Therefore, even though he couldn't allow his dogs to know it, their words had piqued his interest in Ciara.

"Yo, Dom, I never said anything else about shawty after you missed her at the cookout, but I'm telling you, boy, you missed something special," Tremaine said and whistled while shaking his head, exchanging knowing glances with the others in the room.

"Word?" Dominique asked, raising his brow in a questioning manner.

"On my mother, nigga. And you already know how much I love me some Mama Red," Tremaine said, eyeing Dominique seriously.

Looking around the room as he allowed Tremaine's statement to simmer in his thoughts, the head nods he encountered were proof that Tremaine had given him the indisputable truth. Then hating to go against his word but deciding that, in this case, doing so could be beneficial, he mumbled, "Call Sabrina and tell her I'm trying to link up with ol' girl."

"What was that?" Tremaine cupped a hand over his ear and leaned closer with a big grin. Though he had already heard him loud and clear, he asked, "Would you mind speaking up, Dom? I couldn't hear you."

Narrowing his eyes into slits, Dominique sucked his teeth and snapped, "Nigga, call Sabrina and get the damn number, a'ight? There, I said it." He cut his eyes in the direction of the smiling faces around him.

Laughing at his man's obvious discomfort, Tremaine immediately reached for the phone and began punching numbers before Dominique changed his mind.

Chapter 16

Leaving one of the locations that Agent Jones had informed her of in the notes he had complied and given to her, as far as Ciara was concerned, they hadn't come any closer to solving the case than they had been the entire time she'd been in Atlanta. Therefore, as she quietly rode shotgun while Sabrina navigated, she felt somewhat down in the dumps.

Ciara was beginning to second-guess her abilities for the first time since her arrival in the city. Though she had spent her entire life—at least the portion of it where she could make intelligent decisions—preparing for a career as an FBI agent, lately, it seemed as if she wasn't good enough for the job. Sure, she had led her class in every phase at the Academy, making excellent grades in martial arts and marksmanship training, but becoming an agent and working in the real world just wasn't as alluring as she once thought it would be. So, for that reason alone, she was finding it hard to continue as if nothing was bothering her.

"Girl, you a'ight?" Sabrina asked, seeing the strained look on Ciara's face. She was neither trying to impose on her nor be nosy, but she wasn't accustomed to witnessing the look she saw on her partner's face.

"Yeah, I'm just fine," Ciara replied, sounding more defeated than sincere.

Cutting her eyes suspiciously in Ciara's direction, Sabrina instantly decided that something had to be bothering her girl, and they needed to talk about it. So, reaching to turn down the volume on the radio, she concluded that unlike Mario Winans and Puffy's rendition of "I Don't Want To Know" that flowed through the Bose system, she *did* want to know, and she planned to know real soon. However, the vibration of her phone and the voice on the other end quickly changed her plans. "Hey, boo-boo," she answered.

Sabrina's voice carried unmistakable love and affection that instantly grabbed Ciara's attention. Though she had no idea what the caller had said on the other end, the sultry giggle that escaped Sabrina's full lips was proof that whatever it was had been music to her ears.

"Oh, he does, huh?" Sabrina asked, turning her eyes in Ciara's direction. "What brought about the change? Because we both know that he doesn't normally do that."

Though Ciara wasn't trying to listen to the one-sided conversation, she couldn't help but hear it.

"Tremaine, now, you know you need to quit." Sabrina found whatever he had just said to be hilarious. "Hold on then. I'm gonna let you ask her yourself."

Hearing that last statement but unsure whether Sabrina had been talking about her, Ciara was completely caught off guard when she held the phone out to her. "What?" she asked, looking at the cell phone like it was a poisonous snake or something else just as vile.

"Girl, take the phone. Tremaine wants to talk to you."

Frowning while wondering what he could want with her, she reluctantly grabbed the phone. "Hello."

"Ciara . . ." He allowed her name to linger on his tongue. "How the hell are you, mama?" he asked coolly with a smile in his voice.

"I can't complain because no one would listen if I did." She laughed, letting go of her previous sullen mood.

"Yeah, I guess you're right," Tremaine said, laughing too. "Well, Ms. Ciara, do you recall my mentioning a friend named Dominique?"

"Uh . . . I do think I vaguely remember you speaking of him." Then responding to his question, she shot Sabrina an evil look.

"Okay, then. I asked because I kind of mentioned you to him, and he's interested in meeting you."

"Look, Tremaine. I appreciate your friend's interest and all, but—" she began.

Hearing the rejection in her voice, he cut in and began to talk fast to salvage the situation that suddenly seemed to be spiraling out of control. "Ma, listen to me. You've got to hear me out. My man is too real, ma. The two of you were made for each other, and I was not just thinking of him when I made this call. Believe me, you need to meet him just as much as he wants to meet you."

Exhaling, Ciara hoped that Tremaine didn't think differently of her after hearing her answer. She liked him, and the last thing she wanted to be thought of was stuck up. But with everything going on right now, meeting someone was the last thing she needed to do. "Tremaine, as I was saying, I appreciate the good look, and I'm sure that your man is a perfect catch, but due to personal baggage, I'm afraid I will have to decline the offer. Thanks a million, though," she informed with more enthusiasm than she actually felt. "Take care, and here's Sabrina."

Not even waiting for a response, she handed the phone back to Sabrina and turned up the volume on the radio. She had heard more than enough of their conversation, and right now, all she wanted to do was end her long work week, retire to her quiet hotel room, and soak in a whirlpool full of bubble bath.

Ending her call, Sabrina glanced over at Ciara and quickly looked away from the accusing eyes that glared back at her. "Hey, I'm telling you now, I didn't have anything to do with that, Ciara. If you need to be mad with anybody, Tremaine is the one, not me . . ." At a loss for words, her voice trailed off.

"Yeah, I guess you're right," Ciara agreed, releasing the eye-lock she held on her friend. "But I'd appreciate it if you would tell Tremaine that I'm not interested in his friend, or anyone else, for that matter. Could you do that for me, Brina?"

"I got you, girl. It's not a problem." Sabrina gave her an understanding glance. However, it was just a characteristic of Sabrina's chemical makeup that just wouldn't allow her to let go that easily. "But, um, Ciara, before I do that, you need to know that Dominique is not only the most gorgeous Black man I know—besides Tremaine, that is, but he is also rich beyond belief."

At a loss for words, Ciara's eyes lowered into slits as she exhaled and folded her arms across her chest.

"What? I was just saying—" she began.

"Sabrina, don't say anything else to me. Take me to my hotel, and I'm good from there."

"Well, damn. Bite my head off for trying to help your evil ass," Sabrina said while inwardly smiling. She enjoyed harassing Ciara, but what she really wanted was for her girl to get some. The bitch was trippin' lately, and Sabrina knew that nothing cured what ailed Ciara better than a big fat dick. The only problem was that she knew what the cure was, but she had no idea how to administer the medication.

"Are you *serious?*" Dominique questioned in disbelief.

"As a heart attack. She flat-out declined, man. I'm telling you, she ain't interested at all, Dom." Like Dominique, Tremaine too was in denial. Neither of them was accustomed to rejection.

"Damn, Dom. I'm sorry to hear that, man," Treon announced. The sad voice he used caused Pimp and Money to chuckle.

"Man, what the fuck is so funny?" Dominique snapped, looking in their direction and causing them to cut short their laughter and avert their eyes. Although he was far from a spoilsport, he felt he had been the butt of their jokes long enough.

"Chill, player. It's not that serious, nigga," Treon said. "Shawty's bad and all, but at the end of the day, she's nothing but another bitch, so don't trip."

"Nigga, I ain't trippin' off no ho," Dominique hissed through clenched teeth. "Fuck her," he added, standing and removing his keys.

"Yo, you out, shawty?" Tremaine asked.

"Yeah. I've got a few things I need to handle before I hit the club tonight. Look, I'm gonna check you niggas later, a'ight?" Still angry but unsure why, he strolled out of the room with everyone's eyes glued to his back.

Giving one another startled looks as they watched him exit, Treon shrugged his shoulders and concluded that whatever had gotten into Dominique would undoubtedly be worked out when they met him later. So, putting the whole scene behind them, they continued their little festivities as if nothing had ever occurred.

Meanwhile, as Dominique drove out of Treon's exclusive suburb, the only thing that continued to course through his mind was, *Who is Sabrina's friend?* And even more so, he couldn't help wondering what type of female she was to have declined his advances when she had to know that, like Tremaine, he too was very wealthy. He couldn't figure it out, but suddenly, he found himself liking this Ciara character a whole lot.

Chapter 17

"Where to, miss?" the cabdriver asked, peering over his shoulder into the backseat at the young lady who had just entered his vehicle.

Racking her brain for the restaurant's name, Ciara could only recall the street it was on. "Um . . . Virginia Avenue, please," she replied, leaning back in the seat.

"Okay, then. Our next stop will be Virginia Avenue," the driver, an older Black man, announced jovially while pulling the cab away from the hotel.

Relaxing in the comfortable seat, Ciara couldn't quite figure out what had possessed her to come back out when she had planned to spend the evening in a tranquil state.

"Dom, are there any last-minute arrangements you need me to make in preparation for you and your crew tonight?" Sue was always on point, and tonight would be no different.

"Uh . . . let's see," Dominique said, thinking out loud. "Place a fifth of Absolute in the freezer for Pimp. He likes his vodka ice cold. And make sure to have a velvet rope placed around our table because even if my crew does like to sit in front of the stage, we can at least simulate the privacy of the VIP lounge."

"All right, that's not a problem," Sue informed.

Glancing down at his watch to determine just how long it would take him to pick up his food, make it home, shower, change, and return to the club, he exhaled and replied, "Sue, I honestly have no other ideas. I'm on my way to eat right now, though."

"It figures," she laughed, adding, "There's no rush, so handle your business and bring your ass on."

"Damn, that's how you talk to your boss? The man who signs your check?" he questioned, acting incredulous.

"Man, please. I just called you 'boss,' but you *know* who runs this place. Now, where are you going to eat?" she asked, changing the subject.

"Spondivits. Why do you want to know?"

"Hmm. Of all the restaurants in the city, why do you have to go there? Dom, you have *got* to bring me some snow crab legs, an order of fried flounder, and some fries." Her mouth instantly began to water at the thought of receiving her favorite meal from her favorite restaurant.

"Bye, Sue."

"Dominique, don't you hang up on me," she yelled into the phone.

"Man, I got you. Damn." He smiled. "Fall back, a'ight?"

"Yeah, whatever. Just hurry up and bring my food."

"Look, I'm out, ma, but I'm gon' bring your food through before I head home. I'll call you back when I reach the club." He ended the call and placed the phone back into his pocket. He could see the restaurant from where he sat in traffic. With only a block more to go, the thought of food made his stomach growl.

"Thanks for waiting, sir. I promise that it won't take but a moment," Ciara informed her driver, stepping out of the cab. Glancing at the restaurant's name as she headed toward the entrance, she realized why she hadn't recalled it. The European pronunciation made it so much easier to think of the street name instead.

Entering the establishment and immediately remembering the process she and Sabrina had followed when picking up their orders, she gave her best award-winning smile. She spoke to the middle-aged Black female behind the cash register. "Excuse me, Ms. . . ." glancing down at the lady's name tag, she corrected herself. "I mean, Mrs. Jordan. I'm here to pick up an order. The name is 'Valentine.'" She reached inside her Coach bag for her wallet.

"Valentine . . . Valentine . . ." the woman said, peering down at a pad. "Okay, here we go," she stated, returning the smile. "You ordered broiled and fried shrimp with Spanish rice, clams, and a lobster tail, am I right?"

"Yes, that's exactly what I ordered, but can you add a large, sweet pink lemonade to that, please?" Then retrieving her wallet and removing the amount of money needed, Ciara noted the gracious look that the woman wore as she quickly moved off to see to her order. Watching her, it instantly hit her that the courteous behavior she experienced in Atlanta was, for the most part, absent in her hometown. That, if nothing more, was one of the things that drew her to the bustling city.

Suddenly, the loud thud of metal colliding with metal drew her attention to the outside. Covering her mouth in shock at the view she saw through the glass, Ciara all but forgot her food as she rushed out the door.

"Man, I don't believe this shit," Dominique shouted while banging his shoulder against the inside of his door, trying to get it open. Thanks to the cab that had backed into the driver's side of his Mercedes, the door was crushed.

"Oh Jesus, I'm so sorry! I . . . I didn't see you," the unnerved cabdriver exclaimed, massaging his temples as he shook his head.

With a loud crunch, Dominique nearly fell out of the car due to the force he had exerted to jar the door open. Exiting the car and observing the damage to his newly purchased S550, his shoulders slumped. He was extremely upset, and there was no getting around the fact that his new toy was ruined. Regardless of the miracle that bodywork could perform, he concluded that he would never drive the Benz again after today. Thanks to the accident, his car, attitude, and day had all been ruined.

"Sir, I swear, I didn't see you in the rearview mirror," the cabdriver babbled incoherently, drawing Dominique out of deep contemplation.

Taking a deep breath, Dominique tried to calm his anger before speaking. "Never mind whether you saw me. The damage is done. I need your insurance information, if it's not a problem."

"Oh my God, is everyone all right? This is all my fault," Ciara blurted out, staring from the two twisted vehicles to the distraught cabby with sorrow-filled eyes. "If I hadn't had you out here waiting, this would never have happened."

Wondering who the female voice behind him belonged to, the only thing running through Dominique's mind as he turned around was that he didn't have time for this shit. But as he laid eyes upon the woman's face, his angry frown quickly disappeared, replaced with a dumbfounded grin.

Rambling on in her haste to apologize for what she felt was partly her fault, it took Ciara a moment to register the look upon the handsome face that openly stared at her. However, as she blinked to clear her vision, her sparkling gray eyes widened in recognition. Inwardly smiling as her mouth hung slack, she thought, *It can't be him*. As quickly as the thought arrived, the smile that made his handsome features even sexier clearly stated that the man before her was the same one who had been haunting her dreams.

Chapter 18

With the accident and freak encounter behind them, Ciara and Dominique had relocated. Deep in conversation as they lounged in Houston's, one of the city's most exclusive restaurants, eating the house specialty of Hawaiian steak, Ciara truly enjoyed the easy flow of their verbal intercourse.

"Do you like your steak?" Dominique asked, biting his lip and intently staring into her eyes.

"Yes, it's truly delicious." Although she tried to hold his stare, she failed. His eyes were entirely too intense, causing her to shift uncomfortably in her seat.

Snapping out of the meditation he had been in as he swam in the endless pools of her bluish gray eyes, Dominique couldn't help comparing his dinner acquaintance to a much thicker, more delicious version of Alicia Keys. Swallowing the saliva pooling in his mouth at the thought of devouring her whole, he averted his eyes and spoke to release the sexual tension in the air. "I'm sorry that you never had the opportunity to get the meal you had ordered from Spondivits. But I'm hoping that this makes up for it."

Glancing from his sincere eyes to the smorgasbord that lay in front of her, Ciara honestly doubted if the meal she had left behind could begin to rival the one before her. Even so, the conversation and mutual connection they had made in such a short time were well worth any loss she could have possibly suffered. "No, please. There's no need for you to be sorry. The meal is superb," she said, placing her napkin on the table and releasing a breath to simulate just how full she was.

Smiling at what he felt was a cute gesture, Dominique still found it hard to believe that she—the woman he had chased through a crowded club—was really in his midst. Relishing the smile that lit up her face in response to his own, he chuckled slightly and shook his head.

"What?" Ciara questioned, intensifying her beautiful smile as she playfully tilted her head.

"No, sweetheart. I'm not laughing at you, Cee. I was thinking of just how ironic it is that you're actually here with me. I mean, after missing each other in the club, I didn't expect to bump into you again."

She too felt that their meeting was indeed ironic. But ironic or not, even though Dominique's words had her blushing like a schoolgirl, she realized that letting her guard down and allowing him easy access into her world would be foolish. Therefore, when they met in the restaurant parking lot, as much as she wanted to give him her real name, for some reason, "Cee" came out instead of "Ciara."

Noticing how she had seemed to drift off into thought after hearing his revelation, Dominique subtly cleared his throat and pushed his chair back. "Um, Cee, is every-thing okay?"

"Yes, I'm fine," she said, returning to the present. "That was just such a sweet sentiment, Deon, and I'm not accustomed to receiving those."

"Oh, is that so?" Dominique gave her a skeptical look, but inwardly smiling, he wondered why he had given her the name "Deon" instead of one of his more exotic aliases. However, fine or not, until he found out whether she was a gold digger or a maniac, "Deon" would remain his name.

"Yep, it sure is!" She playfully returned his skeptical glance.

"Well, in that case, I personally take on the task of presenting you with every bit of the sweetness you've been denied thus far." Swelling his chest out and receiving a sexy giggle for his efforts, he said, "From now on, think of me as your personal 'candy man.'"

"So you say?" Ciara asked. Though she wasn't quite aware of the sultry tone that her voice had taken on as she unconsciously ran a manicured nail seductively over her bottom lip, the idea of so much "chocolate" at her disposal was a welcome thought.

"No, I promise." His firm response jarred her out of her mental appraisal.

"Okay." Ciara sat back in her seat, blinking to clear her head. "Let's be realistic. Although the food and conversation have been great, and we both concluded that there was a strange but mutual attraction the first time we laid eyes on each other, isn't this a little too soon to be making promises?"

Though his dark eyes revealed teasing humor, Dominique's face was void of emotion when he hunched his shoulders and said, "I can't say. I've never done this before, so I guess I'm not quite sure of the official waiting period or rules governing promises." Inwardly smiling, he plucked an uneaten shrimp from Ciara's plate and leaned back in his seat to await her response.

Opening her mouth to reply but not quite sure of how to go about doing so, Ciara, instead, chose to fold her arms across her chest and think about it. Though it felt like minutes had come and gone, only a few seconds had lapsed, with the two of them holding eye contact before bursting into laughter.

However, quickly regaining her composure, Ciara was the first to speak. "All jokes aside, Deon, I really like you so far, and I'm glad we had the chance to meet formally. But I will be honest with you, so please don't take this the wrong way. The last thing I'm in the market for is promises, a man, or the problems that come along with one."

"Okay," Dominique said, reaching for his glass of Bacardí Limón. Although his demeanor remained cool and calm, his mind reeled from her disclosure. This was far from what he had expected. A woman usually wanted everything she could get from him, while he took the necessary steps to duck any commitment. Thus, hearing such words from a female was unexpected.

"However, what I do want is a friend, and there's no need to be afraid of my becoming too attached." Smiling at the raised brow stare he held her with, Ciara playfully flicked her tongue and announced, "Now, if you're willing to let your guard down and allow me to be myself, then I want you for a friend."

Playfully nodding his head, little did he know that his boyish smile and the sexy dimples that framed his smooth, handsome, downright pretty eyes had already won Ciara over. She had wanted him from the first moment their eyes had locked upon each other months before. And regardless of what her mouth said, now that she had placed her talons in him, she wasn't about to let him escape her grasp.

Chapter 19

Glancing up from the papers she was busy going over at the sound of Ciara humming, "If I Had One Wish," Sabrina wondered what the hell was going on. Ciara usually carried a chip on her shoulder the size of a boulder, and the last thing that Sabrina was accustomed to her doing was humming a song, especially a love song.

Tossing Sabrina a casual glance, then smiling, the twinkle that emanated from Ciara's bright gray eyes was magical. As she cut her humming short, she said, "Hey, girl, I hope you had a blessed weekend."

Little did she know, she'd piqued Sabrina's curiosity to the point of no return. "Uh-uh, girl." Sabrina grinned foolishly, closing the folder she had been going through. "You have got to tell me what's gotten into you. And before you try to say it's nothing, don't even pull that shit, 'cause I know when you're not yourself." Then quickly getting up from her chair, she crossed the room and perched on the edge of Ciara's desk.

"Damn, ho. Back your ass off my desk," Ciara giggled. She was amused by the way Sabrina sat there staring at her as if she wasn't budging until she received some answers.

"Well? Spit it out, trick, and don't leave anything out either," Sabrina ordered.

"*Excuse* me?" Ciara gave her partner a fake look of indignation.

Frowning, Sabrina shot her an accusing look and hissed under her breath.

"A'ight. Damn. I met somebody. You happy now?" Ciara stated flatly. However, her smile defined just how happy she was.

Sabrina's mouth fell open on hearing the cause of Ciara's jubilation. Then, quickly recovering, she said, "You're lying. When did this happen? Who is he, and why haven't I met him yet?"

Ciara's smile was etched into her face as she began to answer each of her friend's questions. "Well, first and foremost, I'm telling the truth. Second, we were properly introduced a few weeks ago, but strangely, we met months before when you and I went to Club Kaya. His name is Deon, and if you must know, you haven't met him yet because I gave him a fake name, and I'm trying to decide whether he's worthy before you get a chance to see him." She lowered her voice and averted her eyes after supplying the last bit of information.

"Uh-uh. You not giving this nigga the goodies all this time and lying about your name? Now, that shit there is so damn ghetto," Sabrina snickered.

Ciara popped her tongue in disgust and snapped, "Ain't no goodies jumping off, and I'm far from ghetto. See? That's why I didn't want to tell your ass, bitch."

"Don't we get in our feelings quickly when a nigga gets us open?" Sabrina teased, bringing a smile back to Ciara's face. "Well, if you haven't been giving up the goodies, then what the hell have you and this Deon been doing for the last few weeks? 'Cause you damn sure ain't humming and smiling for nothing."

"Girl, *everything*." Ciara closed her eyes dreamily. "We do things that I haven't done since I was a teenager. I mean, Sabrina, he's so sweet and romantic."

Clapping her hands excitedly, Sabrina exclaimed, "He's sweet and romantic. Okay, now, tell me more."

"A'ight, let's see. We had a picnic lunch, sitting on a blanket in the middle of Piedmont Park. We've gone bowling at Glenwood Lanes, shot pool at Tight Pocket, and skated at Cascade Skating Rink like two teenagers."

Giving Ciara a stink look, Sabrina asked, "Does that nigga have any money? 'Cause all the stuff you called off sounded rather cheap, if you don't mind me saying so."

"O-o-o-oh! Sometimes you just—" Ciara began to berate Sabrina with an angry look.

"Bitch, I was just playing with you," Sabrina chuckled, cutting Ciara's response short. "I like the dude already, wit' his romantic ass. So, go ahead and tell him your real name and get it over with so your girl can meet him."

"Yeah, that's more like it then," Ciara said, twisting her neck in a stank fashion. "Don't talk about my man. And for the record, his paper is long as hell."

Smiling, Sabrina announced, "Say that, then. That's your man. He's romantic as hell, he's got plenty of paper, and I hope he's fine," Sabrina said, giving Ciara a questioning look and receiving an affirmative nod. "Uuh-huuh," she drawled out the word purposely before giving Ciara a high five and adding, "Girl, you better give that nigga some ass."

Seriously considering doing just that, Ciara bit her lip in thought, then waved her hand dismissively in Sabrina's direction and started humming her song. However, as she did so, she just couldn't stop thinking about Deon. Therefore, she wondered where he was and what he was doing at that very moment.

"Olivia, you're not hearing me, ma. I can't make it. My schedule is booked up." Peering at his Ebel watch, it was apparent by the blank look on his face that Dominique wasn't trying to be bothered.

"But, Dominique, I've already reserved your favorite suite at the Radisson. As we speak, my fingers are beneath the lace lingerie I'm wearing and are slowly inching their way into the opening of my pussy." Moaning softly, she spoke in a pouty voice. "Darling, don't make momma waste all this sweet cream on her fingers. Please, clear your schedule and come make me happy."

Sitting up straighter in his seat, Dominique was forced to swallow at the thought of Olivia's words and actions. Drumming his fingers on the desk, he was tempted to go and needed sexual satisfaction. But common sense stated that even though she possessed the necessary tools and tricks to sate him physically, it was Cee he truly yearned for. As bad as his "little head" wanted to accept the invitation, his "big head" won out.

"Nah, baby. As much as I'd like to take you up on your offer, I'm sorry to say that I ain't gon' be able to do it." He lied, yet he told the truth since he had promised himself that he would stay away from other women for once and designate all of his time and attention to Cee.

Abruptly changing her whole demeanor after receiving his refusal, Olivia flew into a tantrum. "Dominique, why the hell are you doing me like this? I give you whatever your heart desires, and I've done so for over a decade, yet you dismiss me like I'm nothing. So why must you do me this way, huh? Tell me, goddamnit!"

Remaining calm and composed, Dominique barely spoke above a whisper. "Olivia, retain some semblance of control. You're in a state of disarray, and it's neither cute nor becoming. Now, as I was saying, I'm not going to be able to make it, but—"

"But my ass, Dominique. Now, who the hell is she, and what makes this bitch so damn special that you won't come to me? Baby, don't do me like this. It's been nearly a month since you fucked me. I *need* it, Dominique, and damn you, I need it *today*."

Having heard enough, Dominique hissed, "Listen to me, you cum-crazy bitch. I'll fuck you whenever and *if ever* I decide to. Furthermore, don't question me or my motives where another woman is concerned because I won't answer you or any other whore. Now, do I make myself clear?" he asked, lowering his voice to barely above a whisper.

"Ye . . . ye . . . yes." Her voice cracked as a torrent of tears rushed down her face. "You . . . you make . . . yourself clear."

"A'ight, then. So go home to your rich husband and fuck him. Oh, and before you go, I'll be busy for an undisclosed amount of time, so don't call me. I'll call you."

"But, Dominique . . ." she whimpered more than called out.

Dominique had said everything he had planned to say, and he had no intention of hearing anything more from her. Therefore, he ended their call by removing the receiver from his ear and quickly allowing his attention to return to more important business.

On the other end, Olivia dropped the phone and balled up in a fetal position as her loud wails filled the bedroom and suite. Her cries were loud and racked her body, and the worst part was that she was genuinely hurting. She loved Dominique with an intensity that bordered on being fanatical, and for as long as she could recall, all she really wanted was him.

That being the case, she had done everything she could to elevate him to his present status, hoping they would be together. However, upon obtaining riches, instead of getting her man, he suddenly seemed to be moving further out of her clutches.

Concluding that something had to be done about their situation—and soon—she decided to find out who the woman was—and do away with the problem. There could be no distractions, so regardless of what had to be done for her to have Dominique all to herself, it would be done. She hadn't placed her life, marriage, and livelihood in jeopardy on many occasions just so another bitch could reap the benefits. So, as she wiped her tears, Olivia mumbled, "Dominique, at times, you can be so cruel. But no one, and I do mean *no one,* understands or knows you better than I. This, my love, is why we will *always* be together, regardless of whether you want me."

Her tears poured nonstop, but Olivia smiled brightly.

Chapter 20

Glaring across the net and expanse that separated the two of them, Ciara crouched in a defensive stance with her racket firmly gripped in her sweaty palms. Waiting for Deon's serve, her heart raced with excited anticipation.

"Hey, shawty, I hope you're ready for this one 'cause I'm about to bring the heat. I'm sorry to tell you, but to win, I've got to pull out all the stops on this one, love."

"Whatever, nigga. Would you just serve the freakin' ball and save the conversation until after I beat that ass?" Smiling, Ciara stuck her tongue out to taunt him further. She only needed one more point to win, and by all means, she planned to get it.

"Okay, you asked for it." Smirking, Dominique tossed the ball in the air and sent it speeding across the net.

Ciara worked the court like a Wimbledon champion, grunting loudly as she used every ounce of her strength to send the ball flying back across the net with each of his return volleys. They had been at it for hours, and although her muscles ached and sweat drenched her Reebok halter top and matching skirt, she was truly in her element. She was not only enjoying the exercise, but she was also happy to have found someone who shared her passion for the game that her father had taught her when she was a child.

"Shit," Dominique exclaimed, tripping as he ran to intercept the line drive shot that ended any hopes he may have had of winning the game.

"Yes," Ciara screamed in victory while jumping up and down. "I whipped that ass, now, didn't I?" She sashayed across the court to where he lay sprawled on his back.

"Yeah, you got that," he grinned. However, as he watched her coming toward him, he realized that regardless of the game's outcome, he had won. The sight above him was delicious, and he couldn't contain the instant erection that popped up as soon as he saw the dark hairs that stuck through the damp, lacy panties as she proudly stood over him with a hand gripping her rounded hip.

"Yeah, champ. What you got to say now?" she questioned, staring down at him with one of her brightest Cover Girl smiles.

Unable to speak for fear that his voice would give him away, Dominique instead returned her smile and subtly licked his lips at the outline of her phat pussy and the enormous yellow ass cheeks that he was able to see from the front. Her thickly formed thighs afforded him just enough of a gap where they met in a V to see through them to what he felt was the promised land.

Sweeping her long ponytail over her shoulder and using the back of her hand to wipe sweat from her brow, Ciara squinted at the blazing sun and asked, "So, what are you planning to do? Lie out here all day and sulk over your loss? Or move on with your life?" Biting down on her bottom lip as she rubbed his defeat in, she thought that he was the most gorgeous creature in the world as he slowly began to stand.

Grinning, he replied, "Well, I guess since you put it like that, I may as well get on with the rest of my life. So, for starters, give me some of that good sugar." Then reaching for her, he lowered his lips to hers and embraced her tightly.

"Um-m-m, boy, quit it," she protested in a whiny, girlish voice.

Ignoring her words and delving his tongue into her mouth where it roamed freely, Ciara reluctantly squirmed out of his grasp as his large hands found their way beneath her tennis skirt and kneaded the flesh of her ass that had spilled from beneath her panties.

Breathing heavily, she placed a hand on his chest to distance them. "Whoa, now, baby. Slow down," she said, exhaling a nervous breath.

Clasping his hands together, he gave her an affectionate peck on the lips and stepped back. He smiled inwardly and noted how her breasts rose and fell with her labored breathing. The way her extended nipples pushed against the material of her top also stamped what he already knew. She too was horny as hell, and her resolve weakened after a month of slowly wearing her down.

"Look, I'm . . . uh . . . going to get cleaned up. I . . . um . . . won't be long," Ciara stuttered and quickly walked toward the house. Though she wasn't quite sure why she hadn't succumbed to his skillful physical tactics yet, as she made her way up the cobblestone walkway to the house, she realized that she wouldn't be able to hold out much longer. They had been playing the cat-and-mouse game long enough. Therefore, with that thought in mind and the fact that she was moist and throbbing for some loving, she decided that instead of using the shower in one of the guest rooms like she had been doing, today, she would shake things up a bit.

Watching Ciara exit through unblinking eyes, Dominique followed each sway of her gloriously rounded hips and gently shimmying behind. Even now, after spending every conceivable moment with each other, she had a way of captivating his attention like no other female had ever done in his 30 years.

Though at the moment it was her body that held his gaze, in no way had he fooled himself into believing that her outer beauty was the cause of his unwavering interest. He had been with some of the most beautiful women in the world, so the icing on the cake, so to speak, when it came to her, was her brains, lust for life, and the attentiveness that she genuinely showered on him. All these things packaged together had easily placed her on a pedestal above any other woman who had held his attention before her arrival.

Nevertheless, although she embodied all these qualities, Dominique was experiencing sexual withdrawal like nothing he had ever known. And even after using every imaginable ploy in his trick bag, nothing had assisted in getting her to give up the drawers. Deciding that he would just have to continue his pursuit, he adjusted his rigid erection and slowly began to walk toward the house. With each step he took, he hoped they would soon consummate their relationship because he didn't know how much more teasing he could stand.

Chapter 21

Ciara's heart beat out of her chest as she stood naked beneath the soothing nozzles that shot jets of water at various speeds. Each showerhead was meticulously positioned so that they massaged different parts of the anatomy.

Though she was nervous at her bold move, she had to admit that the closet-size shower she now stood in was impressive. Not only were the dozen or so showerheads that surrounded her in the brown and beige granite and glass enclosure unusual, but Deon also had a couch that had to measure no less than seven feet and a forty-two-inch plasma screen built into the wall. In Ciara's book, the shower alone had given new meaning to stuntin'.

As she adjusted the gold knobs to find the desired water temperature, she began having doubts about what she was doing. Did she *really* want to let him claim her body after maintaining abstinence for such a long time? With her mind telling her one thing and her body something completely different, she found herself in a stalemate of sorts.

Thinking that by now he was somewhere near and there was no way for her to undo what had already been done, she figured, *To hell with it.* So, as she used the large sponge to lather her body with herbal soap, she nervously concluded that she would allow the pieces to fall where they may. If all else failed, she could always disappear after their coupling and go back to living her life like he had never even existed. This thought and the realization that he only knew her as "Cee" helped to stabilize her nerves . . . somewhat.

Suddenly, the noise she heard in the adjoining room caused her chest to rise and fall with a new emotion that had been absent for entirely too long. Ciara was suddenly experiencing an intense form of anticipation. Now, she only hoped that Deon would follow the path she had laid out for him.

Entering the enormous bedroom, the sound of the shower running along with a trail of clothing strewn across the carpet stopped Dominique dead in his tracks. He was in utter disbelief, yet the smile that swiftly distorted his features as he leaned forward and picked up her panties indicated what was going through his mind. The last thing that he needed was a more vivid proposition. Finding the pair of panties on the floor was more than enough of an invitation as far as he was concerned.

Quickly discarding his clothing on the way to the bathroom, he was as naked as the day he was born when he reached his destination. As he received his first glance at Cee's body through the mist-covered glass, no other frame mattered to him.

Seconds into his observation, the weight he felt between his legs drew his eyes away from the shower to the massive slab of flesh that bobbed between his thighs. Grinning at the pendulum that hung only inches from his knee, he hoped she wouldn't be spooked by its size like so many others had been before her. He would be gentle if she allowed him to make love to her. In fact, as he reached for the doorknob while staring at the yellow globes of her big, juicy ass, there was no doubt in his mind that as soon as he began to work his magic, she would *beg* him to fuck her harder than she had ever been fucked before.

Feeling a slight draft, Ciara turned and came face-to-face with Dominique. Maintaining eye contact, she remained rooted to her spot as the hand holding the sponge dropped to her side.

Dominique's eyes roamed appraisingly over every inch of her body as he stepped closer. Her hair hung in long, wet waves that framed her angelic face. Her mouth was slightly parted, giving her full pink lips a glazed and succulent look. Yet, it was her perfectly formed D-cup breasts tipped with long, thick brown nipples and large areolas with prickly little goose bumps that received his first touch.

Hearing her slight intake of breath as soon as he palmed her breasts and lifted them toward his lips, Dominique whispered, "You're even more beautiful than I imagined." He ran his long tongue teasingly around her left areola. The moan that escaped her throat as her fingers raked through his short, curly hair spurred him on further.

Throwing her head back, Ciara was in a blissful state as she felt him slowly alternate between each of her breasts. His pace was perfect, and with each lick, suck, and gentle bite of her painfully erect nipples, he placed as much of her breast in his mouth as he possibly could and sucked with abandon. This act brought forth low whimpering moans, making her juices flow unrestrained down her inner thighs. The strong hands she suddenly felt on her ass moving in concert with his mouth caused her to rise on her toes and arch her back as a long, thick finger slid inside her. Her breath quickened, and her head spun at the pleasurable feelings she was experiencing.

Lifting her easily, Dominique received no argument as he carried her to the couch. In fact, he was somewhat surprised by the effortless way she wrapped her long legs around his waist and sought out his lips with her own as he sat on the edge of the couch with her on his lap. There were so many things that he wanted to do to her, but at the moment, his erection and heart rate were raging. Therefore, before he could explore her body further or make love to her, he needed to fuck her. Breaking their heated kiss and staring deep into her bottomless gray eyes, he whispered, "Cee, I need to be inside you. I can't wait another minute."

Staring at him with sex-glazed eyes, Ciara wrapped her arms around his neck. Removing her legs from around his waist, she placed the balls of her feet on the couch on either side of him. Never blinking or averting her gaze, she rose upward, using his strong, muscular shoulders for support as she hovered over his huge dick. Slowly lowering herself, her voice trembled upon making contact with the plum-sized head. "Please don't hurt me, Deon!" Completing her statement, with pleading eyes and her mouth wide open, she slowly began to sink on the dick.

"S-s-s-s . . . Shit . . ." Ciara whimpered and winced in a mixture of pain and pleasure as she lifted her body upward.

She had only made one attempt at lowering herself on him. Still, after covering six inches and struggling to do so, chances were that the remaining inches would be a herculean task like no other she had ever undertaken.

Biting down on her bottom lip to suppress her cries but not quite accomplishing the task, Ciara held her ankles apart as high as she could while Dominique beat the pussy up with short, electrifying strokes.

They were soaked with sweat after hours of sexing each other. The muscles in Dominique's torso were coiled bands of steel beneath his tight, chocolate skin.

Grunting as she tossed her head from side to side, Ciara's voice took on a crazed tone as she yelled out, "Fuck me harder." As soon as her words rang out, she bucked her body up hard, using her hips in powerful winding motions to feel his length as deep inside her as he would fit.

Having full access to her pussy due to the position they were in, Dominique grit his teeth and increased the speed and depth of his strokes as Ciara placed her legs over his shoulders and dug her long nails into his back. Oblivious to the painful scratches, his mind registered nothing but her earsplitting screams and the feel and sound of his flesh meeting hers.

"Uh-h-h, baby, damn. Um-m-m . . . make my pussy come," Ciara yelled, adding, "Nigga, work that dick." She was close to coming, and from how her walls trembled, she was sure that her orgasm would be like no other she had ever experienced.

"Oh . . . my . . . God," Dominique groaned, reaching the bottom of her core.

"Oh . . . Oh-h-h-h, baby, I'm com . . ." Pulling him down on her sweaty, convulsing body, Ciara's words trailed off as her juices spewed forth like lava.

Unable to hold on any longer, Dominique grunted, shooting his load deep inside her womb.

Except for their heavy breathing, neither Ciara nor Dominique stirred. After hours of having sex in every conceivable manner and position, they were not only sated but also exhausted. So, as the sun's rays disappeared, leaving only darkness in their wake, they held each other tightly and drifted off into a deep sleep.

Chapter 22

Waking before Dominique, Ciara quietly slipped out of bed and found an extra robe and slippers in his vast, walk-in closet. Donning the large robe and leaving the dark bedroom, searching for the kitchen and some refreshments, she was surprised when her eyes set upon an elevator. Giggling at the thought of someone's house being so big that they needed an elevator, she shook her head and headed for the stairs instead. Taking them two at a time, she was excited and felt like a little girl without a care in the world. She truly felt like a heavy weight had been lifted from her shoulders.

Halting her steps and slowly scanning the area, her gut feeling told her she wasn't alone. As her eyes adjusted to her dark surroundings, she suddenly realized that the growling white shapes slowly moving toward her had to be Deon's prized possessions, Onyx and Sapphire. Ciara wasn't afraid of animals. She had owned numerous dogs in her lifetime and loved them since she was old enough to know what they were.

With no possible escape open to her and Deon nowhere near to call the deadly beasts off, she knelt on the steps and called out to the dogs in a calm voice. "Onyx and Sapphire, come to mama." Then holding her arms out wide, she raised her voice a few decibels. "Come on, now. It's time to eat, and I need you girls to help me find the kitchen." She paused to see if her words had affected them, and the sudden silence signifying that their growls had ceased gave her the necessary confidence to stand.

The first dog padded over to her and began to smell her. Its sister followed and repeated the first dog's actions. Then giving them time to acquaint themselves with her scent as well as that of their master due to the sweat he had left all over her, Ciara began to rub their shiny white coats. They were both beautiful dogs.

"I see that you met my two bitches," Dominique announced, standing at the top of the stairs with his arms folded across his chest. Smirking, he didn't know how she had won them over, but in this case, he was glad that they hadn't performed the one task they had been trained for since birth . . . killing.

Immediately sprinting up the stairs at the sound of his voice, the dogs fought for his attention, leaving Ciara to stare in their wake jealously. "Excuse me, but, um, do you plan to show me some love, or are you going to give those two ghetto bitches all my shit?" she teased, pushing her lips out in a pout.

Laughing, Dominique strolled down the steps and draped an arm possessively around her shoulders. "What are you doing out of bed, and what did you do to my girls?" he questioned, nodding down at the animals.

"I was hungry to answer your first question. But as far as those two whores go," she teased, rolling her eyes at the dogs, "I just had a conversation with them about you, and they recognized my gangsta."

"A'ight, they recognized your gangsta." Pulling her to him for a quick peck on the lips as they headed down the steps, Dominique inwardly smiled at the fact that she was amid killers and had no idea of the danger surrounding her.

After grabbing a snack, a quickie in the shower, and changing her clothes, Ciara explored the massive house with her newfound friends, Onyx and Sapphire, by her side. Roaming the many rooms and endless halls of the ultramodern plantation-style mansion, she figured that by the time she finished her tour, Deon would be dressed and ready to go.

Then coming to a locked room, Ciara's part-nosy, part-investigative side kicked in. Knowing that she was wrong but unable to stop the urge, she tossed a glance over her shoulder, peered down at the impatient dogs that moved back and forth around her, and retrieved a bobby pin from her hair. Looking over her shoulder once more to ensure they were alone, she placed the pin in the lock and worked it around like she had been taught in the Academy. Then hearing a click, she looked down and stated, "Stay here and watch for mama." She turned the knob and entered the room. Locating the light switch, she didn't know what to make of the scene before her.

The room had been reconstructed into a laboratory of sorts. Except for a specially made wood and glass case that seemed to contain every handgun and assault rifle imaginable, and some that were beyond anything she had ever seen, the rest of the room was outfitted with pressure sprayers, a state-of-the-art computer, and what she pegged as microwave ovens of some sort.

Taking a closer look as she traveled farther into the room, it was suddenly clear that whoever worked in this room created masks. And from what she could tell from the samples that lay about, the masks weren't mediocre by any means. These masks had been created professionally, and if worn correctly, their disguising ability would change the wearer's entire appearance.

"I could have sworn I locked this door," Dominique announced in a matter-of-fact tone, causing Ciara to jump.

Giving him a false smile as she turned to face him, she thought, *How could you let him catch you, stupid?* However, in her most sincere voice, she said, "Nope, it was unlocked when I turned the knob." Then turning away from him so that her lying eyes wouldn't be revealed, she added, "You have an impressive arsenal of weapons."

"Do I?" he replied flatly, staring at her closely as she crossed the room.

"Yes, you do." Answering him in the same tone he had used, she tossed him a smile over her shoulder.

"So, what do you see that's impressive?" he asked, placing his bulging arms over the platinum and diamond cross and chain that hung over his chest.

"Hmm-m-m, let's see. For starters, I like that SureFire L72 laser-sighting model and E2D Defender flashlight attachment you have on that SU-16C short barrel with the folding stock. What are you loading in that, .223 shells or 5.56 x 45 mm shells?" she asked, turning to face him with a sarcastic smirk. She also folded her arms across her chest, holding his unblinking stare.

Breaking his stare first, Dominique whistled and shook his head as an infectious smile covered his face. "Damn, ma. *You're* the impressive one. How do you know all that shit?" Surprise was written all over his face.

Smiling also, Ciara announced, "Let's just say that I'm a daddy's girl, and my father is a high-ranking Navy SEAL colonel." With that said, she winked and sashayed to the door and into Dominique's arms before asking, "Baby, did you make those masks?" It was only after the question had been asked that she noted the change in his demeanor.

Pausing unconsciously, Dominique said, "Yeah, I made 'em. Why?"

"Oh, there's no special reason. I just think that you have lots of talent, that's all."

"Well, in that case, thank you." Then as if nothing odd had taken place, Dominique's smile quickly returned. "A'ight, you ready to go, beautiful?"

"Yep, I'm with you, handsome."

"Then let's be out," he said, turning to reach for the light switch.

Using his lull in attention to her advantage, Ciara allowed her trained eye to sweep the strange room again. By the time he found the switch and hit it, bringing instant darkness, she had completely engrained every inch of the room in her memory.

However, as they headed down the hall hand in hand, for the life of her, she couldn't figure out why the room, masks, guns, or anything else dealing with her new lover would weigh so heavily on her mind. Therefore, concluding that she was tripping, she decided to leave the agent in her at work and enjoy life during her off time.

Chapter 23

Pulling up only moments behind the yellow K1200R BMW motorcycle and its two riders, the driver of the souped-up Dodge Charger quickly began to screw on the long-range attachment and infrared lighting device that would give him the clear shot that he so badly needed.

Watching through beady, unblinking eyes as the pair got off the bike, he raised the device to his face and carefully focused on the unsuspecting couple as they slowly removed their helmets. As soon as he caught sight of the long hair that fluttered from beneath the passenger's helmet, he compressed the tiny button and began to shoot a flurry of photographs.

The man's name was George Brooks, and in the city of Atlanta, through hard work and a reputation for never leaving a stone unturned, he had become the most sought-after private detective of the rich and famous. However, more so than the vast amounts of money he had amassed, he actually loved his job and the power it gave him over other people's lives.

As he finished the last shot, he smiled, realizing that his client wouldn't be happy with the photos he had obtained. In fact, if they had any particular interest in the handsome gentleman who possessively held on to the beautiful female, he could imagine they would be furious.

Regarding the pair once more as they exited his line of sight, he laughed, reached for the cell phone lying in his lap, and pressed the digits that would contact his client. Waiting for an answer as he unloaded the photos, Brooks heard the aristocratic voice he had anticipated. Placing a level of authority in his otherwise meek voice, he informed, "I'm parked outside of Club Paragon, and I've just encountered Mr. Valiant and . . . uh . . . his significant other."

"Deon, why do you have me up in a strip club?" Ciara questioned, holding on to Dominique's hand tighter as they made their way through the tightly packed club and people who tried to get his attention. Though the noise level was so high that she couldn't quite hear their words, she could have sworn that the people were calling him something other than "Deon." Then, to make matters even stranger, the huge bodyguards and other staff treated Deon like royalty when they entered the establishment through the velvet rope, leaving behind a long line of people who also wanted to get in.

Though Dominique had heard her question clearly, his only response was a smile and a comforting grip on her hand. There was nothing left to say. All her questions would be answered soon enough. But as he led her through the crowd toward his scheduled destination, he couldn't help wondering whether he had made the right decision.

As she rolled her eyes at his lack of response, Ciara's eyes were drawn to the many beautiful women who paraded around the club in various stages of undress. Locking eyes with a pretty female with a mouthful of platinum and diamond teeth and wearing expensive men's attire, she was shocked to see that the she-male was receiving a lap dance. Yet, what surprised her more was the wink of an eye and the long, rapidly flicking tongue the pretty female gave her as she massaged the bulbous globes of the stripper's ass.

She glared at the woman in distaste, but her thoughts on the lewd act were disrupted when she bumped into Dominique and realized he had stopped. Slowly turning, she heard him loudly announce, "Everyone, this is my girl, Cee. Cee, these are my partners."

Seeing the looks on the faces that stared up at her, Ciara's smile slowly began to fade into a cheesy, panicked frown. Peering from the table back to her knight in shining armor, she wanted to disappear. She just couldn't fathom that these would have to be his friends out of all the people who populated Atlanta.

Sabrina was so caught up in watching Strawberry's performance on stage that she had been in no rush to acknowledge Dominique's new lady friend. But as she turned from the show and received her first glimpse of Ciara, she spat her drink across the table. She was in shock, and from the look she saw reflected in Ciara's eyes, she knew she wasn't the only one.

Looking at Sabrina and then sweeping his eyes around the table at his snickering friends, Dominique raised his brow and stared at Ciara questioningly.

But before he could seek answers, Tremaine loudly exclaimed, "I see that you refused to take no for an answer, so you went out and found Ciara on your own." Then grinning after his announcement, he added, "I'm glad to see that you reconsidered your previous decision and decided to give my boy, Dominique, a chance after all."

At the mention of Dominique's real name, Ciara instantly noted the fake smirk he tossed her. Suddenly realizing they had both been playing the same game, she no longer felt any misgivings about the situation. Instead, rubbing her man's head affectionately, she smiled and replied, "I'm also glad that I changed my mind and decided to give your boy, *Dominique,* a chance, Tremaine."

Deviously cutting her eyes at Dominique after pronouncing his name a little louder than necessary, she released her hold on him and sat at the table. "Okay, we all know each other, so I'd appreciate it if you niggas would quit staring at me like I'm some sort of appetizer or something," she said, directing her words at Money, Treon, and Pimp.

Hunching her shoulders at the laughing trio, Sabrina's only response to the new development was a chuckle, a high five to Ciara, and another long taste from her personal bottle of champagne. As far as she was concerned, now that she knew Dominique was Ciara's mystery man, she couldn't have been happier. Of course, this was nothing more than what she had planned to do initially. However, as much as she tried not to let on to the other members of their little party, her attention was quickly redirected to the stage and Strawberry's sensuous movements. And like the Destiny Child's song that Strawberry moved her fabulously proportioned body to, Sabrina too began to lose her breath.

Seeing the comfortable way Ciara interacted with his crew, Dominique had to admit that he liked her style. So, with that thought in mind and the knowledge that they had all begun the party without him, he slid into the seat beside Ciara and gently placed his hand on her jean-clad thigh.

Feeling his touch, Ciara abruptly cut short her conversation with Tremaine and turned to face Dominique. Immediately noticing his dimpled smile and pretty white teeth, she leaned into him for a deep kiss. The truth had been revealed, and their connection remained intact. As their kiss intensified, they were oblivious to everything and everyone around them.

Chapter 24

Ciara blinked to clear the early-morning film that clouded her vision and turned to receive her first morning glance at Dominique. Since moving in, this had become her ritual whenever she awoke. However, quickly finding his spot in bed empty and ascertaining that he hadn't slept there during the night, she immediately became alarmed.

As she turned her head toward the clock on the nightstand, her perplexed expression turned into a dumbfounded gaze when she saw the time. The only thing that ran through her mind as she glimpsed the early hour was where the hell Dominique could be, and who would he be with at 6:00 a.m. if he wasn't with her?

Slowly working herself into a jealous rage, Ciara tried to recall portions of the previous night. The only problem was, every memory she attempted to recollect brought her back to one particular moment, and after that . . . there was nothing. She could only remember drinking one apple martini that he had made for her, and although she did have a slight headache, there was no way that one drink could have gotten her drunk. Puzzled, she could only draw a blank about the rest of the night, and as she glanced down at herself, she found it odd that she was stark naked.

"Hey, sleepyhead, I was just coming to wake you up for work," Dominique stated, jarring Ciara from her silent vigil. Then giving her his boyish, heart-melting smile, he dropped down at the foot of the bed and yawned.

Lowering her eyes as she stared at his naked, wet back, Ciara's mind was attempting to decipher the situation she now found herself in. She didn't want to jump the gun and overreact, but it was suddenly becoming hard to figure out whether she imagined things or if something was really wrong.

"Baby, can you dry my back off for me?" he asked, removing the towel around his waist.

Reaching for the towel as she rose on her knees, Ciara reluctantly obliged him. At this point, she hovered between being angry and unsure why, so she decided to play it by ear.

"M-m-m-m, that feels so good, baby." Leaning forward, Dominique placed his head in his hands and exhaled. "I've been up working in my study all night, and I'm tired as hell right now," he informed her.

Raising her brow and breathing easier for the first time since awakening, Ciara mumbled, "Is that so?"

After noticing the stress etched into her beautiful face, Dominique tossed her a defensive look. Then his look softened. "Yeah, boo. After you collapsed on me, I was forced to find something else to focus on. So, I caught up on some overdue work, lost track of time, and decided to shower in one of the guest rooms to keep from waking you."

His story added up, and suddenly, Ciara felt foolish for ever having doubts about him. Therefore, as she leaned forward and gave him a soft peck on the lips, she made an unspoken oath to give him the benefit of the doubt if anything like this ever occurred again.

Grudgingly breaking their kiss, Dominique entwined her long, silky hair in his hand and massaged her head as he stared into the depths of her eyes.

"What?" Ciara questioned, breaking their stare and suddenly realizing that the temperature in the room had increased a few degrees.

Dominique repositioned his muscular body on the bed. His reply was another more sensual kiss. However, this time, he worked the tip of his tongue into her mouth when he began to twist her nipples.

Emitting a low, guttural moan, Ciara met his tongue with her own. As their kiss intensified, between his skilled mouth and roaming hands, she was melting and needed the long, hard rod she now stroked with both hands.

"M-m-m, damn . . ." Dominique groaned. His breathing increased as he watched her frantic movements. He knew what she wanted, and like her, he too needed to possess her. So, biting down on his bottom lip to contain himself, he noted that if the time on the clock were correct, she wouldn't be making it to work until late.

Usually a stickler for promptness, as Ciara sped down Interstate 85 in her newly purchased BMW Z4 with the top down and the morning breeze cascading through her damp hair, for once she couldn't care less that she was unfashionably late. After romping in the sack with her man and receiving her early-morning dose of dick with an extra serving in the shower, she was invigorated. In fact, even now, her nipples still stood erect, and the walls of her pussy hadn't entirely calmed their erratic spasming.

Nearing her exit, yet unable to get Dominique and the delicious sight of his ripped body poised and bucking on top of her out of her mind, she fought the temptation to turn around and go back for another round. However, no matter how tempting the thought, common sense and the reality that she was no longer a reckless youth with no responsibilities quickly set in. Changing lanes and flooring the sleek sports car, she raced down the off-ramp and fell in behind the many other commuters who made up the downtown traffic.

The Richard B. Russell Building stood only a few blocks from where Ciara sat cooped up in traffic. She knew how crazy the city streets could be in the morning, so she adjusted the stereo system to V103 and leaned back in her seat to listen to *The Russ Parr and Olivia Fox Show*. Although the wide, bright, and beautiful smile covering her pretty face was a normal sight in the last few months since she and Dominique had met, she had become painfully aware of an astonishing fact for the first time. With a fluttering head and her dazzling gray eyes wide behind the Azzaro shades that covered them, it was clear to her that she had fallen in love. Now, the only question was, did Dominique love her back?

Chapter 25

Buttoning his diamond cuff links and adjusting the starched Cesare Paciotti shirt tailored to drop over his muscular torso just right, Dominique removed his Versace blazer from the hanger and put it on. "Now that's more like it," he announced while admiring his reflection in the mirror that covered the entire wall of his large walk-in closet.

Turning to the antique table and the jewelry box in the middle, he glanced at the gleaming and glittering contents within before deciding. He concluded that his diamond bezel Cartier with a bevy of stones lining the platinum band would perfectly match his otherwise stunning look. So, fastening it on and spraying a layer of sheen over his tight, professionally cut curls, he leisurely exited the room.

Retrieving his iPhone as he moved through the house with Onyx and Sapphire mysteriously appearing at his side, he quickly punched in a series of numbers. Hearing the voice he desired, his tone was firm, low, and straight to the point when he spoke. "It's me," he said. No further acknowledgment was necessary. Sensing the surprised intake of breath on the other end, he continued. "I told you I would get back to you when I was ready. So, now, I'm ready. It's 10:18. Meet me at my favorite spot at noon and have everything prepared to my specifications. Now, is that clear?" he asked with a level of authority in his voice.

"Yes. I'll be there, and everything will be just as you like it, daddy."

"A'ight, cool. I'll see you at noon." After ending the call, Dominique opened the door from his state-of-the-art kitchen, a culinary dream, into his five-car garage. Gliding more than walking, he lightly bit down on his lip as his eyes looked over the canvases covering each car. They were all dream machines, but being as meticulous as he was, he had to pick the right vehicle to match his outfit and mood. Therefore, as he removed the tarp from the chrome-on-chrome sports car that he had only driven on two other occasions, the smile covering his face proved that he was more than happy with his choice.

"And that there would be the home, or should I say, *castle,* of Mr. Christopher Douglas III," Sabrina informed, pulling up to the intercom system at the gated enclosure that blocked their forward progress.

Whistling, Ciara looked in awe at the house and grounds looming ahead. Though Dominique and Tremaine's homes had been sights to behold when she had first laid eyes on them, the residence before her could only be compared to a photo she had seen in one of the tabloids that had shown Oprah Winfrey's mansion. Hearing someone answer the intercom, Ciara pulled her eyes away from the impressive view and turned in her seat to face Sabrina.

"Uh, yes . . . We're Agents Jordan and Valentine with the FBI, and we scheduled an appointment last week to meet with Mr. Douglas today," Sabrina explained into the black box. Waiting for a response, the long silence that followed was tense.

"Enter the grounds, and someone will meet you when you reach the house." The intercom went dead, only to be replaced by the low buzzing sound of the electronically activated gates opening.

Following instructions, they drove through the gates and pulled up to the entrance of the enormous dwelling. And as promised, before they had come to a complete stop, the enormous double doors opened, and a butler in a white tuxedo exited and stood stiffly on the porch.

"Damn, these muthafuckas are paid for real. They even get their own 'Mr. Bentley,'" Sabrina mumbled under her breath as she exited the driver's side.

Snickering at her partner's silly humor, Ciara followed closely on Sabrina's heels.

Standing as still as a statue until the two women were only feet away, the butler spoke in an authentic English accent. "My lord cannot see you for reasons beyond his control, but my lady would like to meet you in the parlor. Follow me, and please close the manor door behind you."

Giving Ciara a questioning look as she raised her brow to meet the raised brow that Ciara wore, Sabrina mouthed the words, *"My lord and my lady? What the fuck is he talking about?"*

Covering her mouth to keep from laughing out loud, Ciara playfully popped Sabrina on the shoulder and hurriedly tagged along behind the white butler.

Reaching the parlor and waiting until the butler had gone to retrieve his "lady," as he'd said, their nosy sides instantly kicked in. "Uh, girl! Look at this big, pretty-ass piano," Sabrina exclaimed, quickly crossing the room and posing against it. "If I had my phone, I'd make your yellow ass sit down and recreate that Alicia Keyes's video. You know which one I'm talking about, right?" she questioned with a serious look.

Flicking her middle finger, Ciara said, "Fuck you," and turned her attention to the walls and paintings that adorned them. Although she did resemble Alicia

Keys, and the snow-white piano was beautiful, she was tired of always being referred to as Alicia's twin. Plus, Dominique had the same piano in his home. However, as she paid closer attention to the paintings and the artists' signatures on each one, her mouth and eyes widened at realizing what she saw. Before her, if the paintings and signatures were authentic, she easily saw over $30 million in the artwork. Yet, there were more.

"Only three of those particular pianos are in North America, and the paintings were a vast waste of money," the regal-sounding voice announced. Instantly garnering the attention of her guests, she expected and was accustomed to the surprised looks that passed between them.

"Um . . . We're sorry for being nosy," Ciara said with a smile. "But your house is exquisite, and we've never seen anything like it." She couldn't help staring at the lady of the house. Mrs. Douglas was far from what she had expected. She wasn't just beautiful. She was breathtaking.

"Please, you have absolutely no reason to apologize. You've done nothing wrong," she said, playfully waving Ciara off as she came farther into the room.

Joining the gathering, Sabrina asked, "If there are only two more pianos like this one in America, then where are the other two?"

"Well, that's a good question, Ms. . . . ." She looked to Sabrina for an answer.

"It's Agent Jordan, and this is my partner, Agent Valentine."

"Now, as I was saying, Agent Jordan, I purchased two of them and gave one to a very special friend years ago. As for the third one, I have no idea who owns it."

"My boyfriend has one just like it," Ciara announced, indifferent to the keen look that her hostess gave her.

"Your outfit is gorgeous," Sabrina commented, observing Mrs. Douglas's cute shape. Sabrina had expected an older, aristocratic woman to meet with them, and she never figured that their hostess would turn out to be so delightful to the eye.

"This old thing?" Mrs. Douglas said, peering down at her attire. "Please . . ." She blushed and laughed as her hazel eyes twinkled. "Where are my manners? Please, have a seat. What can I do for you?"

Taking seats, the trio got comfortable and began to converse. Mrs. Douglas had a pressing engagement that needed her undivided attention within the hour, so she planned to hasten this meeting with the two agents. But her first obligation was to find out what the FBI wanted with her husband.

"I'm sorry that my husband wasn't able to make the meeting, but I'll have him reschedule as soon as he gets back into the country," Mrs. Douglas stated. She placed Ciara's number in her Birkin bag and donned her gold-framed Gucci shades as she hurried to the Aston Martin coupe parked in front of their Jaguar XK8.

Receiving a wave right before the car door closed, due to the dark tint that covered the Aston Martin's windows, any other glimpse of the glamorous banker's wife was obstructed as she sped down the driveway.

Locking eyes with her partner and witnessing the same quizzical look on her own face, Ciara muttered, "Now that's one fly-ass old broad!"

"You damn right she is," Sabrina remarked, shaking her head.

Chapter 26

"O-o-o-o-oh, Dom . . . inique . . ." Olivia whimpered, glowering over her shoulder with a contorted look on her face. Then quickly closing her eyes tightly and unconsciously allowing her head to drop onto the pillow with the intensity of her lover's next plunge, she clawed at the sheets and screamed as the tremors inside her combusted with the force of an atomic blast.

Dominique's movements neither stopped nor slowed down with Olivia's fifth orgasm if he had counted correctly. Instead, gritting his teeth and gripping her tiny waist just above the large swell of her ass, he increased the pressure of his strokes to a sledgehammer pace. As expected, Olivia's body began to convulse with her multiple orgasms. It was only then that he pulled out of her phat, juicy pussy and placed his thick, long dick between the crease of her ass. Slowly moving it back and forth so that it would remain hard, he patiently waited for her spasms to subside.

Crying softly as her breathing slowed to her usual pace, Olivia was as in awe today as she had been many years before when Dominique had first caused her body to betray her. No one else had ever brought her to such a sexual plateau. Being the freak that she was, it was only logical that with him fucking her the way that he was, she couldn't imagine living without him.

Deciding that she was ready for phase two of his ploy, Dominique roughly flipped her over and hoisted her legs in the air before forcing them apart and bending them as far back as they would go. Her pussy sat in the air, and the pink center lay wide open so that nothing stood between him and its bottom. Then staring deep into her sex-crazed eyes, he speared the head into her center and groaned loudly as his thick, twelve-inch rod burst through her viselike resistance.

Dressed and ready to leave, Dominique stood at the side of the bed and stared down at Olivia's still form. Sleeping like a baby and snoring lightly, the angelic look on her face was beautiful. He could never quite understand that when it came to her dealings with him, she had everything to lose and nothing to gain. Yet, for whatever reason, she continued to risk her life and everything she loved for the chance to spend time with him. In his opinion, that was nothing more than pure, unadulterated stupidity.

Shaking his head and peering down at her with a look of loathing, Dominique left the room as quietly as he had entered and caught the elevator to the parking deck of the exclusive hotel. Keying the alarm on his Lamborghini Murcielago Roadster, he quickly got inside, hit the automatic starter button, and dropped the convertible top. Within moments, he exited the parking deck and drove down Peachtree Street toward the Underground and his restaurant. He had already contacted his friends and let them know to meet him there. He was in a rush to share the news he had obtained from Olivia with them.

The devious smile that covered his face was proof that, once again, he had used boss game and his well-rounded sexual prowess to conquer and control the heart, mind, and body of the one woman who loved him more than she did herself.

***

The meeting had gone well, and as Dominique gave pounds and hugs to each of his departing friends, his heart swelled with pride as he watched them race out of the lot in various expensive whips. They had all come a long way in life, and with the world at their fingertips, there was still so much more they had left to accomplish. Yet, as Dominique sat in his car thinking back on how it had all come about, he had no choice but to smile as he leaned back in the seat, closed his eyes, and was transported back in time . . .

Summer, 1979

Dominique was thankful he had met and befriended the beautiful older female, Olivia. If she hadn't appeared when she did, he had no idea what may have become of him had he carried out the half-baked scheme he was ready to carry out. But even as grateful as he was, and though she had supplied him with a job, a place to stay, clothes, and all the good loving that a young, impressionable man could hope for, he was still distressed.

This affliction was more due to a bruised ego than anything else. In fact, each night since he had been attacked and robbed of his belongings, he had combed the downtown streets religiously in search of his assailants. Though he wasn't sure how he would deal with them if they were ever to materialize, the brass knuckles he carried in his pocket for added protection would surely give him the edge he needed.

Hearing noise approaching, Dominique hugged the alley wall and immersed himself in the shadows. The loud voices that seemed to be approaching boasted of violent intent and hope for easy prey. Though he couldn't see the group of youths clearly, if his mind hadn't failed him, the voices were identical to those of his attackers. His heartbeat increased, and he swallowed the lump in his throat. He slid his hand inside his pocket and quickly retrieved his weapon, sliding his fingertips into the brass knuckles. He waited for the precise moment before stepping into the path of the approaching crew. Then coming face-to-face with his adversaries, Dominique swung with all his might . . .

Present

Laughing out loud, he opened his eyes, sat up straight in the seat, and pressed the automatic start button, bringing the heavy roar of the Lamborghini's engine to life. Though he seldom, if ever, thought about that night from so long ago, it was that moment in the past that set the fast-moving, breakneck pace for their futures.

However, as he whipped the beast machine out of the parking lot, what he found not only funny but also ironic was the fact that although he had fought with all his might and skill to inflict damage on his attackers, they still ended up beating him to a pulp and robbing him *again*. But refusing again to take the loss, Dominique waited until he had healed and sought the crew out once more for another rematch. It was this foolish yet heroic attitude that wore the young crew down. Deciding that it was just too much of a problem to continue fighting him every chance he got to catch up with them, they reimbursed him as best they could and voted him into the clique. Thus, at that point, Dominique, Tremaine, Treon, Money, and Pimp became inseparable.

At that moment, their lives were changed forever because, little did they know, they had just been sucked into the first phase of Dominique's vision.

Chapter 27

Dominique was not just angry at what had been revealed to him moments before. On the contrary, he was in a rage. However, as he glanced at the photos before him, he couldn't help wondering what it all meant. Was it all just a coincidence? Or had this been orchestrated from the moment they met? The words he heard next roused him from his deep contemplation.

"It seems that this time, your taste for eye candy has gotten you in a bind of sorts." Rearranging the photos and placing them back in the big manila envelope, low, sarcastic laughter erupted from the bearer of the bad news.

Lowering his lids, Dominique glowered at his host. The last thing he saw in the whole dilemma was any humor. His anger threatened to boil over at any moment.

"Look, relax," said Dominique's partner in a cool, businesslike manner. "Don't sweat the small stuff, player. As usual, I'll fix everything on this end. Trust me. We're fine."

"You sure about that?" he asked, speaking for the first time. Due to the circumstances surrounding his partner's reputation, he wasn't quite sure of anything at the moment.

"Come on, now. Do you really have to ask that question? Have I ever let you down before, Dom?" Leaning back in his chair, Dominique's partner wore an arrogant look that pretty much answered any question before he could ask it.

Nodding his head in affirmation, Dominique placed his freedom and that of his friends in the hands of the person who sat on the opposite side of the table. Only, as he saw the sour look that twisted his partner's face, he braced himself for the words he knew were coming.

"Well, thanks to you and your ability to catch and capture an FBI agent for a girlfriend, how about you break the news to your crew that you have cost them millions? The assignment for two weeks from now is canceled. And since I need you far from Atlanta when I put the finishing touches on this shit, you and your little girlfriend must take a long trip. Now, are we in agreement?"

"Yeah, we're in agreement," Dominique replied. Though he hated the tone of voice used to rebuke him, he understood the magnitude of his failure. He had placed everyone in danger, and now he had no idea just how much, if anything, she knew. *Damn you, Ciara. Out of everyone, why do you have to be a federal agent?* This was the only thing that continued to resonate through his mind.

—

Chapter 28

Entering the gates and grounds of Shady Grove Country Club, Ciara slowed her car to a mere crawl as she took in the scenery around her. The grounds were meticulously landscaped, and the snobbish bourgeois stares clearly defined the vast wealth within the gates with which the people she passed held her.

Shaking her head and speeding up in her sudden haste to reach the giant structure ahead, she decided that if money turned people into the phonies that glared down their noses at her, she would rather remain in the position she was already in. With that thought in mind, she rolled her eyes and neck in a stank manner at a group of older, pseudo-aristocratic white women, who, in turn, stared openmouthed in her wake.

Finding a parking space, Ciara grabbed her attaché case and Marc Jacobs's bag and exited her car. Charging up the walkway and taking the steps leading into the country club, she was caught up in the click-clacking sounds her heels made each time they connected with the steps. Then suddenly, she heard her name being called. Turning toward the female voice, she squinted her eyes before placing her arm above them, attempting to shade them from the sun.

"Ciara! Oh, my darling! What brings you to Shady Grove?" Mrs. Douglas asked with a bright smile.

Momentarily pausing at the friendly tone, it wasn't until Ciara shielded the sun from her vision that Mrs.

Douglas came into view. Then recognizing the older, petite beauty before her, she instantly returned the smile and headed toward her. Reaching Mrs. Douglas, she said, "I was on my way to meet with your husband."

"Oh . . . Is that so?" Mrs. Douglas asked, looking off into the distance as if something had grabbed her attention.

Picking up on the abrupt lapse in their conversation, Ciara followed Mrs. Douglas's eyes to the road. Scrutinizing the vehicle that slowly made its way up the winding driveway, Ciara wasn't sure due to the distance that separated them, but she could have sworn that the car was one of Dominique's.

"My husband is actually here, and I didn't even know it," Mrs. Douglas stated, more to herself than Ciara. "Well, I assume that stranger things have occurred." Her laugh was infectious, causing Ciara to remove her eyes from the road and join in.

"Yes, he's here, and I'm running late," Ciara said, looking at her watch.

"Now, we must quickly remedy that. I'd better let you get to your meeting. My husband can be an animal regarding business and promptness, so if you encounter any problems, tell him that I held you up." Grinning, she turned to head back toward the women who had been patiently waiting for her.

Time had already been wasted, and she needed to hurry up and get to her meeting, so Ciara rushed up the steps.

Entering the country club's restaurant and giving her name to the maître d', she was directed to Mr. Douglas's table. The stares accompanying her questioning progression through the dining area caused her to feel uncomfortable. But returning the looks with an aura of confidence that she didn't feel, she held her head high and regally and placed an extra swish in her already shimmying hips.

Regarding the beautiful woman as she moved between the tables in his direction, Mr. Douglas felt a slight stirring in his midsection. Though the stirring had only lasted for a moment, he was caught off guard by her arrival.

Fond of his ability to ignore the fairer sex, Mr. Douglas had easily forged his position in the world undeterred by outer beauty and the promise of sexual pleasures. At the age of forty-five, he owned the biggest, most prosperous Black-owned bank in Atlanta. With holdings tallied in the billions, his personal wealth easily accounted to $800 million or more.

Mr. Douglas stood up and buttoned the first button on his tailored Armani suit. Then seeing her stride quicken as she headed toward him, he graciously pulled out a chair nearest to him and awaited their first official greeting.

Hmmm, Ciara thought, garnering her first glance at the renowned Mr. Christopher Douglas. From what she had read about him in the short bio created prior to their meeting, she had already been impressed. But once more, she'd been fooled by words on paper. She would have to reconsider the idea that only old, boring, fat people could amass vast wealth. In this day and age, the hip-hoppers created the Puff Daddys and Jay-Zs that made young wealth acceptable. So, understanding that she would no longer judge a book by its cover, she quickly surmised that she could see what Mrs. Douglas hung around for. To make a long story short, he was fine.

"Ms. Valentine, am I right?" Mr. Douglas said and offered her an outstretched hand.

"Yes. I'm Agent Valentine," Ciara subtly corrected. Then grasping his hand and taking her seat, she said, "I'm glad you were able to fit me into your busy schedule." Pushing the remnants of an uneaten plate of food away from her, it was clear that whoever had sat here before she did had lost their appetite for some reason.

"No, I'm just sorry that I could not make our last engagement. Unfortunately, business called, so it couldn't be helped. You understand I'm sure." His gaze lingered on her pretty face and her mesmerizing gray eyes that were only rivaled by the hazel eyes of his wife.

Nodding her head in response to his statement, she noted the sprinkling of gray hair that peppered his temples. They assisted in adding a level of sophistication to his already handsome looks. "Yes, I understand completely." Ciara tore her eyes from the older gentleman and placed her attaché case on the table. She was on the government's time; therefore, work was the sole reason she was there.

After an hour and two iced teas, Ciara was basically at the same place she had been before making the acquaintance of Mr. Christopher Douglas III. She was at square one. Quickly concluding that sharing worthless small talk was far from necessary, she placed her notes back in her leather attaché case and stood. It was time to exit.

Mr. Douglas's Southern upbringing wouldn't allow him to send her off improperly, so he stood and said, "Agent Valentine, I'm truly sorry that I couldn't have been of more assistance. As the head of a multibillion-dollar institution, I can't take a hands-on approach where our smaller branches are concerned. However, if our international investigation uncovers anything that may be of assistance to you and the Bureau, I promise you will be the first to hear of it."

"I'm holding you to that," Ciara replied seriously. Though for some odd reason, his smug attitude and the grin that seemed to lie just below the surface caused her to be somewhat suspicious of him, other than her gut feeling, there was really no merit to her suspicions.

Chuckling, he raised his hands in mock surrender. "Whoa, now, Agent Valentine. Remember, I'm one of the good guys."

Ciara grinned. "Sure you are, Mr. Douglas. And for further reference, remind me never to forget that information. Have a nice day." Then grabbing her purse and attaché case, she turned and strolled out of the restaurant.

As he watched her departure, Mr. Douglas's smile instantly disappeared. Though he had always been in the mind-set that beauty and brains never went hand in hand, unless his gut feeling played tricks on his mind, Agent Valentine seemed to be the exception to the rule. As she disappeared, he removed his phone from the pocket of his Armani suit jacket and hurriedly punched in a series of numbers. The phone was answered on the third ring, so he spoke in a flat, no-nonsense voice forgoing any pleasantries. "The situation may be more dire than I thought. I need you to place the utmost importance on my earlier orders."

Chapter 29

"Nah. I'm not going for that," Tremaine said, giving Dominique a look that bordered on a half smile/half frown. What Dominique had just revealed to him was more than his sane mind could fathom. Thus, seeing the solemn look on his best friend's face and finally allowing the enormity of the situation to sink in, he shook his head in disbelief and dropped into the chair. "Now, Dom? How the fuck is this possible?" he asked, cradling his head in the palms of his hands.

"I don't know, man. I really don't know."

Sharing a moment of silence between them, Tremaine was the first to speak. "A'ight, she's a Fed," he announced, raising his head to glance at Dominique. "So, now what? Can Ciara hurt us? And if so, how do we ensure she doesn't?"

Glancing into Tremaine's eyes, it was painfully apparent to Dominique that his man was deadly serious. Measuring his response to ensure that his words weren't taken out of context, he said, "I can't be sure of anything at this point, but I will say that there's no level I won't go to to ensure that our secret remains safe."

"Nothing?" Tremaine raised his brow after asking the question, making his intention crystal clear.

Dominique released a breath but continued to hold eye contact. "Yeah, you heard me. Nothing."

"Cool, then. Now, how about you break the news to me on how this new turn of events will affect the move we have planned because I'm ready to get that money." His expression brightened at the mention of money.

"It's off, dog. Our connect feels that it's too dangerous right now, so we're goin' to pass this one up, ya dig?"

"Hell nah. I don't dig that shit one damn bit." Tremaine jumped up from his seat and began to pace the floor. "Shit, Dom. How can we pass up over $6 million, and we don't even know if we've been compromised?"

"Because I said so, goddamnit!" It was rare that Dominique spoke to any of his crew in such a manner, but the new turn of events caused him to be operating on a short fuse.

Tremaine abruptly stopped pacing and held Dominique with a blank stare before releasing a sarcastic chuckle and shaking his head. "Because you said so, huh?"

"Look, bruh, I'm sorry. It's just . . ." Dominique exhaled. "This shit is hard for me to swallow and all. Man, I'm really feeling shawty."

Tremaine's features softened as he said, "Okay. I got ya, partna. It's off, and that's all there is to it. So now, what do we do?"

"This is where shit gets intricate, so sit down and let me explain how we're gonna work this thing out." Dominique waited for Tremaine to sit, then announced, "The first thing I need you to do is move the lab and weapons to your house while I'm gone."

"While you're gone? Where the hell are you going while—"

"Shh, listen," Dominique said, cutting short Tremaine's remarks. "You need to hear me out because I'm about to take Ciara on a journey, and a lot must be taken care of while we're away. Now, I'm trusting you to handle this shit, so pay close attention, a'ight?"

"I'm wit' you. Talk." Tremaine was more than prepared to handle any task Dominique had in mind. However, the slow smile on Dominique's face made it clear that, as usual, he had concocted another one of his devious schemes.

Chapter 30

Ciara shifted the grocery bag in her arm as she attempted to juggle her purse, attaché case, and the new house keys without dropping her purchases. Inside the grocery bag were the necessary ingredients for a surprise candlelight dinner. She had little doubt that the evening would be delightful between the delicious meal, a bubble bath for two, and an even more scrumptious negligee.

Opening the door and walking inside, her dreamy thoughts were interrupted. Standing guard inside the huge foyer, Onyx and Sapphire's eyes were bright, and their strong stances were alert. Grinning at her two girls, she said, "Hey, ladies. Did you two miss mama?" As she strolled past them, heading toward the kitchen, she heard their paws scraping the marble floor behind her. She smiled to herself. There was no need to turn around since this had become their ritual. They would follow her around the massive house until she dismissed them.

"Bae," Dominique's deep voice reverberated off the walls, "I'm glad you finally made it home. I've been waiting for you."

The tone of his voice caught Ciara off guard, yet the mysterious look in his eyes caused her heart to skip several beats. "Hey, boo-boo. I had to stop by the grocery store and pick up some special items for tonight. What's up, though?" Watching the dogs run to Dominique and lie at his feet, she rolled her eyes, thinking they were like a pair of bitches. They constantly crossed her every time Dominique entered the equation.

"I just missed you," he replied, folding his arms across his broad chest and holding her with an intense stare.

Wondering what the hell was going on, Ciara put the bag on the counter and gave him a forced smile. "I missed you too. So, now that we've gotten that out of the way, how about letting mama know what's on your mind."

Holding each other with unblinking looks, even their silence carried a deafening resonance. Only Dominique's abrupt, bright, sexy smile changed the course of an evening that seemed to be headed toward failure.

Returning the smile, Ciara said, "What? Baby, tell me what the hell is going on."

"If you can get away from your busy modeling schedule for a week or so, I want you to go away with me. What do you think about that?" he asked slyly, watching her closely for any changes in her demeanor.

"Umm, I, uh . . . I don't know what to say." She wanted to scream. There was nothing that she would rather do than run away to the farthest reaches of the world with the one man that she had grown to love with every fiber of her being. But such pleasures weren't within her grasp when she was in the middle of a serious investigation.

"Well, if you don't know what to say, yes would definitely work for me. You have no idea of the vacation I have planned for us. So, what's it going to be?" Dominique smiled, knowing he had her stuck between a rock and a hard place.

Unbeknownst to Ciara, she had a sour look on her face that gave her forced smile a look of despair. The thought of approaching Senior Agent Ms. Craddock and asking for a vacation amid an investigation was unpleasant. Yet, she wasn't about to allow the opportunity that Dominique offered to slip away without putting up a worthy fight.

"Baby, you okay?" Dominique asked, feigning concern.

"Uh, yeah. I was just thinking about your offer," Ciara lied.

"Then you're doing exactly what I hoped you would do." Dominique winked his eye. "So, what's your answer? Because I need to confirm our reservations."

Ciara averted her eyes and bit down on her bottom lip in deep thought. Then pausing to run numerous ideas through her mind, she replied, "Let me see what I can do, and I'll give my answer tomorrow. Will that be soon enough?"

"Yep. Tomorrow will be just fine, baby." Then inwardly beaming, he opened his arms wide and allowed Ciara inside them. As usual, things were right on schedule.

Chapter 31

Peering over the rim of the *Newsweek* she had been reading, Sabrina's gaze fell upon Agent Craddock's door, her boss. In the last hour, she had repeatedly reenacted this procedure, attempting to determine what was happening on the other side. Except for the loud, bickering voices that she had heard thirty minutes ago, things were now too quiet. However, on the verge of being a nervous wreck and not even the one in the line of fire, Sabrina decided that if Ciara didn't come out of the office in the next fifteen minutes, she would investigate.

Before the thought had completely run its course through her mind, the door to Agent Craddock's office opened, and Ciara strolled through the threshold. Sabrina dropped the magazine, grabbed her purse, and snagged her stocking on a jagged screw in her haste to catch up with her partner as they entered the hallway. "What happened?" she asked, scrutinizing Ciara closely. "Tell me you didn't go up in that woman's office and act a damn fool, Ciara."

Ciara smiled, causing the blank stare she had worn to dissolve. "I can't tell you that I didn't act a fool, but let's just say that I was . . . extra persuasive."

"She actually gave you a vacation?" Sabrina squealed excitedly.

Ciara flashed her beautiful white smile and furiously nodded her head in response.

"How did you pull it off? Girl, you have got to tell me what you did."

"I put my press game down on the bitch," Ciara exclaimed, inflating her already ample bosom and causing Sabrina to erupt in laughter.

"No. Really? Tell me how you pulled it off."

"I used my trump card for this one."

"Trump card?" Sabrina's dumbfounded look proved that she was lost. "What the hell are you talking about?"

"Washington, D.C., and my *real* boss, Agent Johnson, is my trump card, trick. So, I had to go over her head and get the necessary authorization for this one." Then reaching for her cell phone as they exited the federal building, Ciara added, "In forty-eight hours, you're on your own, Ms. Jordan."

Sabrina's only response to her revelation was a smile. Yet, as they entered the car and headed out of the parking lot, while hearing the excitement in Ciara's voice as she revealed the good news to Dominique, she couldn't help thinking that somewhere down the line, Agent Craddock would be sure to get the last laugh.

Traipsing through Greenbrier Mall and carrying more bags than any one person should have been allowed, Ciara's excitement threatened to bubble over. Although Dominique withheld the information about where they would be vacationing, he gave her his Platinum Visa and instructions to purchase articles that would coincide with a scorching hot climate and made her turn over her passport. Following his instructions to a tee, she happily placed his Platinum card on the counter of every expensive boutique in the mall.

Having already made one previous trip back to her car to drop off her purchases, it wouldn't be long before she needed to return at the rate she was going. Nevertheless, hefting her heavy bags and pondering just how good she would look in all her new designer garbs, she suddenly caught sight of one store that she needed to visit but hadn't made it to yet. Quickly concluding that no vacation would be complete without sexy lingerie, she immediately made a beeline toward Frederick's of Hollywood. There was no doubt in her mind that she could purchase many freaky outfits in the store that would add even more spice to their already spicy sex life.

Feeling her phone vibrate as she entered Frederick's of Hollywood, Ciara wondered who the caller could be and why they had to be calling her now. "Hello," she snapped into the receiver.

"Damn," Dominique retorted. "I would have thought you'd be glad to hear from the man whose money you're spending." Humor was apparent in his tone.

"Oh, hey, boo." Setting her bags down to free her hands, Ciara smiled brightly and brushed her hair away from her ear.

"Hey, yourself. How's the little shopping trip progressing?"

Grinning, Ciara thought that she had better correct him. "Um, baby . . . The shopping spree is proceeding along just fine. But, Dominique, I think it's only fair that I warn you that 'little' is the last thing this outing has been. In fact, to be perfectly honest, I've done it rather 'big,' if I must say so myself."

"Is that so?" Dominique's laughter rang through the receiver.

"Yeah, daddy. I may have outdone myself this time around." Ciara bit down on her lip in shame at how she had gotten carried away, spending so much of his money.

"Do you, mama? I'm pretty sure that you could never spend all the money that I've got." The laughter had faded from his voice, making the comment hold that much more validity.

"You're so sweet, baby. Thank you," Ciara said in a voice that dripped with sincerity.

"It's not a problem. Now, since I'm sponsoring this extravagant shopping spree that you claim to be over-doing on, flatter me with a visual preview of what store you're in and what they have to offer."

"Oh, baby," Ciara said in her sexiest voice, "this is all the preview you need, so listen closely and hear me good. I'm standing at the entrance of Frederick's of Hollywood, and as I look around, my eyes feast on nothing but a smorgasbord of sensuality."

"That's all I need to hear. Look, I'll deal with you tonight." Then heaving a deep sigh, he groaned, "Hurry up. I'm out."

Laughing at his response, Ciara ended their call and hurriedly picked up her packages to return to the exciting task of shopping. Life was good, and with how she felt at that moment, she was sure that her life could only get better.

Chapter 32

Dominique placed his cell phone back on his hip. His stride quickened as he headed toward the escalator that would take him to his desired destination. If his memory served him correctly, Frederick's of Hollywood was located on the next level, meaning they would arrive in minutes.

Grinning smugly, he turned to face his man, Spanky. Though they would generally be rivals when it came to women, for this occasion, Spanky was the only person he would pick for this job. He looked okay if Dominique's opinion counted for anything. But since women felt that he was gorgeous, placing any form of hatred on the back burner, Dominique decided to test Spanky's player talents.

"Yo, this broad better be a damn dime piece too, Dom. You already know I got a reputation to uphold, my nigga," Spanky announced in a teasing tone as the store they sought came into view.

Smirking, Dominique replied, "Yeah, whatever, nigga. You just make sure to lay the charm on heavy and don't come back empty-handed, you feel me?"

"Do I?" Spanky sucked his teeth arrogantly. "Nigga, if she's got a phone and address, consider that shit mine when I return. Now, which one is she?" he asked, moving the toothpick in his mouth with his tongue.

Allowing his eyes to sweep through the window and store beyond slowly, Dominique locked in on the exqui-

site frame he would recognize from any distance, bringing an instant smile to his handsome face. "There you go,
playboy. She's standing near the counter with tight jeans
and a white tank top. Now, go get her, and I'm not trying
to hear any excuses when you get back, either."

"Whew," Spanky exclaimed, rubbing his palms together. "Uh, uh, uh. Now, *that's* what I call a dime. She's
beautiful. Her hair is long and curly like I like 'em. Plus,
shawty's got ass for days." Slapping Dominique on the
shoulder, he smoothed down his mustache and goatee,
then boasted, "Watch your boy work his magic."

Slinking back out of view, Dominique had a bird's-eye
view of the store, unsure of what would transpire or
whether the end result would have explosive repercussions. He held Spanky with an unblinking stare as he
entered the store and approached Ciara with all the
confidence and charisma he had at his disposal. But
what caused his heart rate to increase as his blood
slowly began to boil was the bright, beautiful smile that
appeared on Ciara's face when she turned and acknowledged Spanky's presence. At that moment, Dominique
wished he had pegged her wrong. Because in the deepest
recesses of his mind, he had hoped that she wasn't the
snake he'd suddenly found her to be.

"Miss, your purchase comes to $439.17. Will you pay
with cash or credit?" the saleslady politely asked.

"I'll be crediting this to my boyfriend's Visa," Ciara
replied, reaching into her purse to retrieve the card.

"Allow me," Spanky said, sliding his Mastercard across
the counter.

"Excuse me?" Ciara remarked, turning around. Completely caught off guard, she couldn't help the smile that
contorted her features due to the audacity of the strange
but handsome man.

Giving her his boyish, dimpled smile, Spanky said, "I would take it as a personal privilege if you would allow me to handle this purchase for you." Then peering into her pretty face and bright gray eyes, he had to blink to remember the true nature of his task.

"Uh-uh," Ciara laughed at the game that dripped from his tongue like molasses. "Come on, now, why would paying for my purchases be such a privilege?" she teased, twisting the corner of her mouth questioningly.

"A'ight, you got me." Spanky threw his hands up in defeat. "I'm a sucker for a beautiful woman, and when I saw you from out there," he pointed in the direction of the storefront window, "I couldn't control the urge that came over me. I just had to come in here and meet you."

"Is that right?" Ciara blushed at what the good-looking stranger had revealed to her. Even though she realized that he was only spitting game, even if the game was lame, his words were flattering.

"Excuse me, but whose card would you like me to ring this order up with?" the saleslady asked, looking from Ciara to Spanky, unsure how to proceed.

"I'll be paying for the lady's things," Spanky informed, taking charge.

Ciara gave the saleslady an affirmative head nod. How she looked at it was that if he was so adamant about spending his hard-earned money on her and receiving nothing in return, so be it. Then too, from his outer appearance, it was clear that money was something that he had no shortage of. However, these days, with all the frontin' and fake flossin' that goes on, diamonds, expensive clothes, cars, and credit cards don't really equate to wealth. The Rolex watch, diamond-studded chain and bracelet that adorned his wrist, and sparkling earrings were nothing more than window dressing as far as she was concerned.

Spanky, closing the gap between them, allowed his eyes to roam over Ciara's prominent frame, mentally undressing her as they traveled their course. Then reluctantly ceasing his observation, he held out his hand and stated, "My name is Spanky. And you are?"

"Ciara . . ." she stated, adding "Valentine" as an afterthought.

"Hmm . . . Ciara Valentine," he repeated the name, allowing it to linger on his tongue before running the tip over his already moist lips. "I like that," he said, grinning slyly.

"Here you go," the saleslady butted in. "I hope you enjoy your purchases, and please come back and see us again." Then locking eyes with Ciara, they shared a knowing glance.

"Thank you," Ciara stated and grabbed the bags. "Thank you too," she said, turning to face Spanky, who had been expectedly staring at her ass.

"Please, no thanks are necessary. I love to spoil my women," he said. His chest inflated with pride at the realization that he had hooked another dime piece for his already overflowing harem. "Ciara, I was thinking that maybe the two of us could go—"

"Look, I appreciate your handling the purchase of my items and all, but this is where we part company." She gave him a sorrow-filled look even though inside, she smiled at the look of utter disbelief on his face.

"Huh?" Spanky mumbled, dumbfounded. "Can I get your number so maybe we can get together for dinner or something later?"

"I'm sorry, I can't do that. I'm in a relationship, and I love my man very much." Then as if the thought suddenly hit her, she added, "You may even know him. My boo owns Club Paragon, and they call him Dom P . . . Dominique Valiant," she said proudly.

***

Watching Ciara and Spanky conversing, Dominique's patience was waning. *What the hell are they talking about?* That thought alone was eating him up. Yet, regardless of how he felt about the circumstance he now found himself in, he had set it all in motion, so whatever direction it took, he would see it to fruition.

Watching the pair closely, it suddenly became apparent that their little meeting of sorts had ended. Ciara exited the store first, strutting with a confident stride and a look that advertised her delight.

Dominique never even took the time to note the defeated look on his friend's face, thinking that Ciara was nothing more than a dirty rat bitch. It was bad enough that she was a federal agent, but then to make matters even worse, she had the nerve to get with another nigga during a shopping trip that *he* was sponsoring.

"Yo, Dom, that's fucked up," Spanky snapped, breaking Dominique's train of thought.

"What the hell you talking about? What's fucked up?" Dominique needed to take his anger out on someone, and the wrong words out of Spanky's mouth could easily make him the recipient of his wrath.

"You're on some straight bullshit, man." Sucking his teeth, Spanky stared at Dominique with malice.

Dominique suddenly realized something wasn't quite right, quickly causing his anger to dissolve. Then his heart began to beat out of his chest for some reason. "What happened, man? What did she say to you?"

Spanky rolled his eyes and answered, "Dom, why the hell didn't you tell me she was your woman? Not only did she call your name out like she was proud as hell, but she also went as far as saying she was deeply in love with you. The worst part is, I even jacked off $439.17 for some damn lingerie you'll be ripping off her ass instead of me."

Shaking his head, he snapped, "You're gonna pay me my muthafuckin' money back too, nigga."

Dominique was stunned. He couldn't believe that Ciara had turned Spanky down and kept it real with him. Nothing made sense to him at this point. Yet, he realized deep down, he had hoped that she would pass this test because caring about her as he did, he wasn't sure how he would have dealt with her deceit had she failed. Laughing at the irony of the entire situation, he concluded that she might love him after all.

Chapter 33

"Tremaine, can this big piece of scrap metal move any faster?" Dominique teased, shooting subtle glances through the mirror at Ciara and Sabrina, who were caught up in their own conversation.

"Ha-ha, muthafucka! I'll have you know that this so-called piece of scrap metal cost me a *very* pretty penny. And furthermore, if you keep running your damn mouth, you and your woman can walk the remaining miles to the airport," Tremaine grinned.

"*Excuse* me?" Ciara blared from the backseat, playfully popping Tremaine in the back of his head. "I know I didn't just hear you threaten to kick me and my man out of your damn truck, punk."

"Ouch, woman. I was only joking. Dom, get your girl, man," Tremaine chuckled, rubbing his head.

"Nah, baby. He ain't got to worry about getting her because if she puts her damn hands on you again, her yellow ass belongs to *me*," Sabrina held Ciara with an evil stare, then burst into gleeful laughter.

The other occupants in the stretch Excursion followed suit. However, unknown to the others, each passenger was caught up in their own thoughts.

Dominique thought of the one thing that had plagued his mind since the first moment it had been brought to his attention. Ciara, the woman he had grown to love, was a federal agent. Though he fought with every ounce of strength he possessed to find a positive remedy to their dilemma, when all was said and done, only one truth remained. Ciara, the love of his life, was the enemy.

Abruptly cutting her laughter short, Sabrina stared out the window into the distance, drifting off in thought as usual.

Tremaine's thoughts traveled in numerous directions as he adjusted the satellite radio. The first thing he wanted to do was hurry up and get Dominique and Ciara to the airport. When they were safely delivered to American Airlines, and the friendly skies would be responsible for their well-being, he would enjoy some mind-blowing cunnilingus from Sabrina. Just the thought of her thick lips on his even thicker tool gave him a semierection.

However, allowing his train of thought to journey to other more important issues, Tremaine, for the hundredth time in the last few days, began to think of a way to claim the millions of dollars that Dominique had all but demanded that he forget. After replaying numerous schemes in his head, he pretty much concluded that they could do it regardless of whether Dominique played a part in the mission. Inwardly smiling, he decided nothing short of a natural catastrophe could keep him from claiming what he felt was already his.

Ciara's smile was stuck to her angelically beautiful face as she leaned farther into the soft leather interior of the luxury SUV. Between the sweet loving that Dominique bestowed on her throughout the night and early morning, along with the ten-day vacation they were about to embark on to an undisclosed location, she was experiencing butterflies. She couldn't recall ever being as excited as she now was.

Yet, neither their explosive lovemaking nor the prospect of the dream vacation could compare with the real reason for her joy. Ciara was a month overdue for her period, and her cycle *always* came on time. Therefore, although she hadn't checked and wasn't 100 percent sure, if she had to bet on the outcome, she would be willing to wager that she was pregnant with Dominique's child. As her smile broadened with the revelation, she had to admit that carrying his baby wasn't a bad idea at all. How could it be when she was in love with him?

Reaching Atlanta International Airport's busy, traffic-congested entrance, Tremaine double-parked and jumped out of the truck to help Dominique with the luggage.

Hefting the heavy Louis Vuitton bags from the back of the truck and placing them on the ground, Dominique glanced toward the side of the vehicle where Ciara and Sabrina were engaged in a flurry of girlish banter. After concluding that the women were out of earshot, he turned to Tremaine, who was busy making eyes at a flight attendant whose shape resembled a Coke bottle. Shaking his head, Dominique said, "Tremaine, let me holla at you for a moment, shawty."

"Yeah, what's the business?" Tremaine asked, reluctantly tearing his gaze away from the gorgeous flight attendant.

Waiting for Tremaine to finish getting his eyeful of the exotic beauty, Dominique said, "I'll be back in ten days, bruh. I need you to handle the relocation of the lab and weapons ASAP." He removed his house key and handed it to Tremaine. "Be sure to feed my girls, Onyx and Sapphire, daily. Sue has already got instructions on what needs to be done with Paragon, so the club won't be a problem."

"I got this, nigga. Just go ahead and enjoy your trip. Damn," Tremaine stated, faking annoyance that he didn't necessarily feel.

"Yeah, I already know that you've got everything in order. But, Tremaine . . ." Dominique said, holding his partner with an intense, unblinking stare. ". . . Remember what I told you. The move we had planned is off; you hear me, man?" He gently gripped Tremaine's shoulder after his question.

Pausing his response longer than necessary, Tremaine averted his eyes from his best friend and said, "Man, I know . . . damn." He gave off a cheery laugh to hide his discomfort.

"Baby, we better get going unless you have another way to get to our destination once we miss our flight," Ciara suggested.

Breaking eye contact and grabbing their bags, Dominique gave him a brotherly hug and a pound. Then the two of them strolled toward the terminal. He couldn't help the look he tossed back over his shoulder in Tremaine's direction. Though his man winked and waved like everything was fine, Dominique had a gut feeling that shit was far from fine. A level of suspicion resided behind his man's smile, and they had known each other entirely too long for Dominique not to have been wary. Yet, as he entered the airport terminal and lost sight of his partner, it was clear that Tremaine would do whatever he had in mind, and there was nothing Dominique could do or say about it.

Ciara held on tightly to Dominique's hand as their plane taxied down the runway. Receiving a smile and a gentle pressure on her hand, she felt the plane wheels leave the tarmac at the exact moment that she leaned her head on his shoulder. Though the plane ride itself was nothing new to her as she had been riding them all her life, this was the first time that she had ever flown with a man—*her* man at her side.

Inwardly smiling at the vivid thoughts that ran
through her mind, and even though she was still unsure
of their destination, she realized that a vast ocean and
a lot of time separated them from their next stop. So,
seeing the first-class section of the plane was somewhat
empty and secluded, she slowly trailed her fingers down
Dominique's stomach and grasped the slab of meat that
instantly reacted to her touch. Then giving him a sly
look and reaching for the blanket to toss over them, she
grinned at the shocked look he wore when he felt her
tug at his zipper and release his length. As she lowered
her head to his lap, her last thought before taking his
dick into her mouth was that this act would undoubtedly
make her a member of the Mile High Club.

Chapter 34

"Oh my God," Ciara exclaimed again for what seemed like the millionth time since their plane landed in Dubai. She had only viewed the city from the air. Yet, even from their altitude above the clouds, the mecca she witnessed beneath her was beyond anything she could have expected in the desert were she not observing it with her own eyes.

"You like it?" Dominique asked, smiling at Ciara's unmistakable look of delight.

"Baby, this place is like something out of a dream," she answered, wrapping her arms around his waist and placing a juicy kiss on his succulent lips. "Thank you for bringing me here, sweetheart. Thank you, thank you, thank you," she repeated while covering his face with kisses each time.

"A'ight, a'ight. Calm down, baby. Let's at least make it out of the airport before you get all dramatic on me," Dominique laughed. He was genuinely happy to see the joy that this vacation was giving her.

"Okay, hold on. Let me catch my breath first." Ciara exhaled and placed her palms over her heart to calm herself. "All right, I'm ready now."

Chuckling, Dominique grabbed her hand and said, "Come here, woman." He reached for his cell phone and immediately began to punch in a series of numbers.

"Yeah, I'm here . . ." Ciara heard him say into the receiver as she surveyed the scene around her. The airport was much grander in décor than any other she had seen in her travels. Marble, glass, and gold were the only materials that seemed to have been used in its construction. Though no examples were necessary to define the country's wealth—had any been needed—all the naysayers had to do was gaze upon the airport and its occupants.

". . . We're exiting the airport as I speak. The car is white, right? Never mind, I see it," Dominique informed the caller, leading Ciara through the multitude of people mulling around in front of the airport. "We'll be there soon . . . Uh-huh . . . You already know how I do it." He laughed. "Yeah, I'll see you then." Ending his call, he led Ciara toward a white Rolls-Royce and stood by as the chauffeur opened the rear door for them to enter.

"Mr. Valiant, I have been instructed to take you wherever you want to go." The chauffeur spoke his best English but had a deep Middle Eastern accent. Closing their door and entering the driver's side, he added, "Your luggage will be forwarded to the hotel. Now, where would you like to go first?"

Peering into Ciara's bright-eyed face, he leaned back in the seat, wrapped an arm around her shoulders, and pulled her close. "Take the scenic route around the whole city, then head to the hotel."

"Yes, sir," was the chauffeur's only response as he pushed the button that raised a dark partition that separated him from his prominent passengers. His orders were explicit; thus, there was no further need for discussion.

Cuddling up to her Prince Charming, not only did Ciara plan to see the city during their scenic tour with the privacy that the dark partition offered them, but she also had a few other things that she needed to see to as well.

***

Halting their lewd acts as the Rolls-Royce abruptly stopped, Dominique raised the curtain covering the window and inwardly smiled at the structure looming above them.

"Oh my . . . Are we here already, baby?" Ciara hurriedly found her discarded panties, put them in her purse, and smoothed her dress.

Dominique smiled at the cute, sly look on her face and replied, "Yep. Time sure flies by when you're having fun, right?"

Ciara's only response to his question was a wink and a knowing grin.

"Come on, beautiful," he said and gave her a soft peck on the lips and opened his door.

"It's about time that you arrived." The voice held a distinct American undertone, but its Middle Eastern origin was unmistakable.

Dominique was barely out of the car when he glimpsed his friend and business partner. "Zu-hari, thanks for meeting us." Releasing Ciara's hand, he briskly covered the distance between Zu-hari and himself, enfolding the beautiful, bronzed female in a tight hug.

Completely caught off guard by the familiarity of her man and the undisclosed female, Ciara's jaw slightly dropped, giving her a confused look.

Zu-hari caught the surprised stare and quickly dislodged herself from Dominique's grasp. "Hello. I'm Zu-hari, and I take it that you are the beautiful Ciara," she said, extending her tiny hand.

Quickly regaining her composure, Ciara took the offered hand, noting the sincerity of the smile that adorned Zu-hari's face. "It's nice to meet you, Zu-hari, and thank you for the compliment."

Releasing Ciara's hand, Zu-hari turned her attention back to Dominique. "I've already taken the liberty of inspecting your quarters, and as I'm sure you already know, everything is up to your expectations. Work calls," she said, peering at her watch. "So, once you have gotten some rest, call me. There are a few business matters that we need to discuss. Enjoy your stay, Ciara, and if there's anything you need while you're here, don't hesitate to notify me." She smiled and swiftly made her way to an awaiting Mercedes and driver, who was adorned in a turban.

Watching as the driver held the door open for his employer, Ciara waited until the door had closed, concealing Zu-hari before she turned to Dominique and asked, "Who is she?"

"I'll explain later," he replied flatly. "We need to get acquainted with our new living arrangements since we'll be here for ten days."

Allowing him to lead her toward the hotel entrance, it was only at that moment that she took notice of the hotel's magnificence. From her position beneath its enormous bulk, she concluded that it easily towered five to six hundred feet. Although that was somewhat unusual, the fact that the chrome and glass structure was built to resemble the rectangular lateen sail of a ship was what made it so incredibly fantastic. However, as she entered the hotel, her mouth immediately hung slack in awe. The beauty she observed in the lobby all but dwarfed any other hotel she had ever entered by far, making it painfully clear that, as Dominique had already warned her, they were truly staying at the only seven-star hotel in the world.

Accepting a glass of champagne and removing a cracker covered with caviar from another tray carried by a richly dressed waiter who strolled regally through the vast lobby, Ciara tightened her grip on Dominique's hand and smiled invitingly. Biting down on her bottom lip in thought, for the first time in her life, she felt as though she was truly living a fairy tale. She only hoped that, like most fairy tales that occur during dreams or in magical faraway lands, hers would never end. But for now, she would gladly take each day slowly, savoring every moment. As far as she was concerned, that was all she could do.

Chapter 35

Dropping her phone on the marble table, Olivia began to massage her aching temples. Thanks to the information she had just received from Dominique's personal assistant, Sue, her head suddenly throbbed violently.

After her instincts had kicked into overdrive telling her that something was wrong after the first few days of endless unanswered calls and unreturned messages, thanks to Sue, she no longer had to guess why Dominique had seemed to have disappeared. It was now painfully clear that he had left her hanging once again. And to make matters even worse, from what she had ascertained from their brief conversation, he was with his newest female companion.

Feeling the first tear escape her eye only to be joined by another, Olivia made no move to thwart their slow progress as they made their way down her face. Instead, allowing her shoulders to slump in defeat as the floodgates suddenly burst, she dropped her head in her hands and released all her pent-up frustration. She was truly hurt, and for the first time in her vivid memory, she gave in to the realization that Dominique had slipped from her grasp.

Experiencing racking sobs at the thought of never living the happily ever after life she had envisioned for the two of them, it was too much for her to rationalize the idea that another woman and Dominique would live that life instead. Thus, as her mind ran rampant, picturing multiple scenarios she couldn't have possibly foreseen, Olivia was so caught up in her visualizations that she failed to hear the approaching footsteps.

Stopping in his tracks as soon as he saw his wife's distress, Olivia's husband slowly backpedaled into the hallway. From his vantage point, he had a perfect line of sight to where she sat slumped on the couch, experiencing anguish of some sort. Though protocol would typically state that a husband was supposed to console his wife when she was in pain, the situation was far from normal.

Olivia had been living with a secret for many years . . . or so she thought. Not only did her husband know about the longtime affair she had been having with Dominique, but he also kept his own set of skeletons in his closet. As he leaned against the wall with his arms folded across his chest and a smug grin on his face, it was funny to him that, as always, he was holding all the aces in the deck. Naturally, therefore, he would undoubtedly come out as the undisputed champion at the end of the game. Yet, the only gambles he'd ever entertained were those he would surely win. The only thing he couldn't seem to understand was how his wife could not realize this after all the years they had been together.

Wiping the tears and snot from her face, Olivia had no idea she was being observed. Had she known that her husband was home, regardless of how hard it may have been to do so, she would have kept her composure at all costs. However, thinking that she was alone and being heartbroken as she now was, it was inevitable that these feelings come to the forefront.

Now that her tears had run their course, three questions continued to beat her brain: *Where exactly is Dominique? Who is with him?* And last but not least, *What are they doing at this very moment?*

Chapter 36

"Baby, how did they do this?" Ciara questioned with a tremor of excitement evident in her voice. Nonetheless, even though she had asked the question, her eyes and attention were directed at the 80,000-gallon saltwater aquarium in the middle of the Al Mahara restaurant, located on the twenty-seventh floor of the Burj al-Arab Hotel.

"You tell me," Dominique replied. "The view is most definitely exquisite." Although, like Ciara, he too had marveled at the architectural magnificence of the aquarium filled with sharks, moray eels, and every array of beautifully colored fish imaginable upon first witnessing the sight years before. In this case, it was Ciara who his comment had been meant for. It was she who held his unwavering stare. And even though he had witnessed her beauty for the last few months, the sight of her sitting across from him with her hair piled on top of her head and ringlet curls framing her face caused his breath to catch in his throat. Thinking that there was no other manner of describing the picture she presented before him, the word "heavenly" escaped his parted lips.

Turning to face him with a beautiful bright smile in place, she asked, "What did you say, baby?"

"Um . . . I was just—"

"Are you prepared to order now, or would you like more time to make your choices?" the waiter asked graciously.

The waiter couldn't have had the slightest idea, but Dominique had been spared from an uncomfortable moment thanks to his arrival. "No," he said, handing their menus to the waiter. "We're prepared to order now. Let me see . . ." He took it upon himself to make their selections. "Uh . . . We'll have the Iranian beluga caviar, live oysters, salmon pâté with sashimi salmon, and enoki mushrooms in the thick sautéed sauce. Also, bring me two rock lobster tails with a selection of vegetables, creamed sweet potatoes, and a bottle of vintage Manzanillo."

"As you wish, sir. Your order will be promptly served." Bowing, the waiter quickly left the table.

Ciara raised her brow questioningly as her mind reeled with the thought of all the food that Dominique had ordered. Then thinking aloud, she sighed, "Could you possibly tell me how we're going to eat all of that?" The meal hadn't even arrived, and the realization of the amount already had her full.

Laughing, Dominique said, "Trust me, baby. We'll eat it. You just wait and see." Yet, the look of doubt she gave him caused his laughter to increase to the point that was infectious. At that moment, the joy that they shared wiped all thoughts of Ciara being an agent from his mind.

Ciara swallowed the last of her wine. Then her face twisted up in a slightly sour fashion. Though she had consumed numerous glasses of the pale amber Spanish liquor, the subtly bitter taste of the Manzanillo was a bit more than her taste buds were accustomed to.

"You okay?" Dominique asked, finding her somewhat intoxicated features amusing.

"Uh-huh. I'm just fine." She smiled. Looking at the empty glass, she added, "It's just that this wine . . . Manzan . . . whatever the hell you call it, packs a hell of a punch."

"Yeah, I know, baby . . . I know." Dominique inwardly laughed and reached across the table to grab her hand. "Would you like to order anything else?"

"No, baby. I've had more than enough. But there are a few things that I need to tell you." She squeezed his hand and looked longingly into his eyes.

Dominique smiled, yet in his mind, he was well aware that whatever weighed heavily on her mind was about to be revealed. Her eyes reflected sincerity like no others he'd ever gazed upon.

"Dominique, I need you to understand that this in no way has any bearing on our relationship, but I still feel as though I must reveal it to you." She lowered her eyes and exhaled.

"What is it, Ciara? Talk to me."

"Baby, I'm an agent with the Federal Bureau of Investigation, and I withheld that information from you for two reasons: One, I'm undercover and made an oath to let nothing or no one undermine my mission. And second, when we met, I never dreamed that I would fall anywhere near as deeply in love with you as I have."

Hearing her confession, Dominique was utterly astonished. Nothing else after she revealed her love for him even interested him. However, what he did find interesting was the fact that she had come clean with him on her own accord. So, recognizing that she continued to ramble on in explanation, he placed his finger over her lips. "Shhh. It's all right, Ciara. I understand."

"No, Dominique, you must let me explain. No one has ever treated me as well and unselfishly as you have, and I feel that I owe you an explanation. Please, baby, hear me out."

Nodding his head in understanding, he was thankful she wanted to lay all her cards on the table. Then wiping a long tendril of hair out of her eye, he quietly awaited her next words.

"Everything I've told you about my family and myself up to this point is true. I'm the only child of a biracial marriage, and my father is a full-bird colonel in the United States Navy. However, now, it gets tricky." She gave a nervous smile. "After graduating from the Academy, I was relocated to the Washington, D.C., office where I've remained for the last two years."

"Well, how did you end up in Atlanta?" he asked.

Sighing, this was the most challenging part for Ciara. Though she had already revealed entirely too much by even admitting to being in Atlanta undercover, to disclose any more information than that would surely crush her oath. But the love she now felt for Dominique made her past oath seem ridiculous in the face of having to keep any more secrets. So, quickly deciding on the issue, she said, "I was sent to Atlanta to investigate a rash of bank robberies that have gotten under the Bureau's skin."

"Oh yeah," Dominique remarked, sitting up straighter in his chair. "What makes these bank robberies so important that Washington seems to have taken notice?"

"There are too many reasons, and the last thing I want to do is bore you with my work." Ciara waved the question off.

"No, believe me, your work could never bore me. In fact, I'm amazed by the prospect that you, my beautiful goddess, are some dangerously elite female 007." Then grinning, he said, "Come on, tell me more."

"You sure you want to know?" she asked somewhat excitedly.

"I'm positive. Now, humor me with your exploits."

"Okay." Giving Dominique her brightest and most beautiful smile, Ciara said, "I'm going to fill you in on everything that has transpired since the moment I was given the case, but when you start getting bored, don't say that I didn't warn you."

Returning her smile with a sly one of his own, Dominique couldn't believe that a different climate, some superb sex on his part, and a few glasses of wine would be all that was necessary to loosen Ciara's resolve *and* her succulent lips. Yet, concluding that he'd take it however he could get it, he removed his drink from the table and sat back in his chair. It was imperative that he get comfortable before she began because he didn't want to miss a single word of what she had to say.

Chapter 37

Dominique was captivated by the view beneath him. From his perch at the large window over twenty-seven stories above the ground, the bright lights of the city below glistened off the surface of the clear blue ocean. This was one of his greatest visual points in the beautiful, bustling city. Plus, with what Ciara had revealed to him and the realization that he had once again outwitted his captors, he truly felt like he were on top of the world.

"There you are. I thought that you abandoned me." Ciara walked up to him and wrapped her arms around his waist before rising on her toes and gently kissing his lips.

Returning her kiss, he caressed her satin-covered behind. Squeezing her ass before breaking their embrace, he momentarily debated whether she or Beyoncé's backside would do more justice to the strapless dress that now adorned his lady's frame. However, upon further scrutiny, it quickly became apparent that there was no comparison. Ciara was killing the competition, hands down.

"M-m-m," Ciara moaned. "You taste sweet, baby. And you're acting a little mannish too, with all these people around us to see." Peering over her shoulder, she released her hold on his waist and reached behind her to pry his hands from her rear end.

"Oh, you know you're wrong," he teased, feigning indignation. Finally, however, reluctantly allowing his hands to be removed from her soft globes, he watched them shimmy through the thin material of her dress. She could have it her way at the moment, but when they returned to their suite, her sweet ass belonged to him.

Pouting sexily, she swatted his arm playfully. "No. *You're* the one who's wrong, boy, and you know it. Oh . . . my . . . God. That is so-o-o beautiful," Ciara exclaimed, seeing the breathtaking view for the first time since her return.

"It sure is, mami." Enfolding her in his muscular arms, Dominique felt her excitement surge.

"Baby, this place is truly magical, and I never ever want to leave."

He stared down into her bright gray eyes. There was little doubt in his mind that she had meant every word she just uttered. Then instantly having a monumental thought, an idea came to mind that would undoubtedly intensify her excitement.

"Where are you taking me?" Ciara questioned, holding tightly to Dominique's hand as she slowly took the steel steps one at a time. Though she felt safe with her man at her side, the wind that whipped her dress up around her thickly proportioned thighs clearly meant that they were outdoors and at a high altitude.

"Do you trust me?" Dominique answered her question with one of his own.

Ciara didn't even have to think about her answer. "Yes, of course, I trust you, daddy. But . . ." Halting her steps at the sudden sound of an engine starting and the loud *"swoosh"* of something above her, her trust suddenly began to waver somewhat.

Inwardly laughing at how she stood rooted to the spot, Dominique tried to keep a straight face but could not wipe away the smile that brightened his handsome features. "Okay, Ciara, you can remove the blindfold now."

Quickly doing as she had been directed, her jaw dropped upon seeing where they were, standing atop the twenty-eighth-floor helipad. She was in awe as her eyes traveled from the 600-foot drop beneath them to the helicopter and pilot who patiently awaited them before reaching the proud figure at her side wearing a smug grin.

"Surprise!" The words were barely out of Dominique's mouth before Ciara's lips and tongue silenced anything else he could have planned to say.

Ciara was enfolded possessively in her man's arms. A smile had remained plastered on her face ever since the moment that they had taken off from the hotel's helipad. However, abruptly bolting upright at the small islands beneath them, she said, "I've never seen so many small islands so close in proximity before. And look at the magnificent homes built on some of them. There must be at least fifty or more of them."

Dominique leaned forward to receive a better view and said, "Those are man-made islands, baby."

"Really?" she questioned with a quizzical glance.

"Yep, really." Dominique pursed his lips and nodded his head. "The development is called 'The World,' and the islands you see beneath us are only the beginning of what has been planned for construction."

"The World," Ciara repeated as if weighing the enormity of the name itself. "Now, *that* sounds like someone has undertaken a huge endeavor."

"Huge is an understatement where this venture is concerned. And to prove my point, let's say that when the whole World has been completed, every country in existence will be represented, except for Israel. Rod Stewart has already paid $33 million for the island of Britain, and it hasn't even been completed yet."

Ciara whistled at the amount of money that Dominique quoted. It was unrealistic for her to think anyone could drop such large sums of money on extravagant luxuries, such as a private island.

"I plan to buy Brazil," Dominique said with a laugh.

"Yeah, right," Ciara laughed as well since she thought he was only joking. However, catching the fleeting sly grin that he quickly covered up, she suddenly wondered if maybe he did possess such vast sums of money after all. But if it were truly possible that he was that wealthy, how did he obtain his wealth? His words interrupted her silent contemplation and the thought of what awaited her next.

Addressing the pilot, Dominique leaned forward and said, "That's enough sightseeing. Take us to the car." Dominique reclaimed his seat next to Ciara after patting the pilot's shoulder and placing a knot of hundreds in his shirt pocket.

Feeling his arms encircle her torso again, Ciara molded her body to Dominique's and made herself comfortable for the return trip to the hotel.

But as soon as the thought of the hotel entered her mind, the feel of the helicopter veering off in the opposite direction caused her to look out the window again. Then staring up at her man, it suddenly became clear that the night was far from over because the hotel wasn't their next stop.

Chapter 38

Ciara had no idea how Dominique had orchestrated the next phase of their evening. However, as soon as the helicopter landed, the car and driver located nearby instantly caught her attention, leaving no doubt in her mind that they were there for them. "Oh, you're full of surprises now, aren't you?" she stated, eyeing Dominique appreciatively.

Giving her a wink, he nonchalantly boasted, "You don't know the half of it. Come on."

Taking hold of his hand, she allowed him to help her from the helicopter before leading her across the platform to the waiting car. Inwardly smiling at the black tint that covered the windows, X-rated thoughts suddenly began to materialize in her mind, causing her to lean against him and gently turn her index finger provocatively against his palm. But what she saw next abruptly halted her actions, along with any thoughts of pleasuring her man any time soon.

"Well, well. If it isn't the happy couple back from their grand tour of the city," Zu-hari smiled brightly as she stepped from the back of the car to greet them. "By your excited smile, I take it that the scenery from the air was to your liking, am I right?" The question was directed at Ciara.

"Yes, it was delightful," Ciara replied dryly.

"Dominique felt the same way when I took him on the aerial tour. But that's neither here nor there . . ." Zu-hari paused as if a particular thought had come to her, bringing about an even brighter smile. "Anyway, that was long ago. So, are the two of you ready to catch Amnesia?"

Suddenly, the night and the prospect of spending it with Zu-hari wasn't such an exciting thought any longer. Although her comment seemed to have carried some subliminal message causing their raucous laughter, Ciara didn't find any humor in anything she had just said. In fact, the more she observed the Middle Eastern beauty, the less reason she liked her—Period. Though some might have called it hatred, Ciara's instincts warned her that the stunningly beautiful female before her had underhanded intentions where Dominique was concerned. At that moment, she decided to watch their gracious hostess like a hawk for the rest of the evening.

"Baby, how do you like it?" Dominique asked, sweeping his arm in a 360-degree arc.

"It's um . . . beautiful," Ciara replied, more concerned with the fact that Zu-hari held on to her man's arm as if he were her sole possession. *This bitch must think I'm stupid,* was the only thing that ran through her mind at that moment.

"Zu-hari, you have definitely done the muthafucka this time, ma! This joint is even more extraordinary than I'd imagined," Dominique exclaimed, hugging her tightly as he lifted her off her feet and twirled her around. "Thanks to you and Amnesia, we'll be even richer in no time."

Returning Zu-hari's excited smile with evil, lowered lids, Dominique's words, and the realization that Zu-hari was not only his business partner but that the club they now stood in also belonged to him, caused Ciara to gasp. Though she still wasn't pleased with another female being close to her man, the magnitude of the elegance that surrounded her not only stole her attention but also took precedence over any petty jealousy that had lingered in her mind prior to his disclosure. Thus, straightening her face and feigning excitement for her man's benefit, Ciara threw her arms around Dominique's neck, kissed him flush on the lips, and said, "This is not only the most exquisite club I've ever seen . . . but Club Amnesia is also something out of a dream. Congratulations, baby."

Locking eyes with Zu-hari as Dominique folded his arms around her, Ciara caught the fleeting look of envy beneath the surface. Though her smiling face said one thing, the eyes that were the windows to one's soul spoke another language. They spoke of jealousy and larcenist intent. So, flashing her a challenging smirk, Ciara knew that the rules to their unspoken contest had been understood and accepted.

"Wake up, sleepyhead. Time stands still for no one," Dominique said, using the remote control to open the heavy floor-to-ceiling drapes to allow the sun's rays to flood the large bedroom.

"Baby, no." Ciara attempted to avert her eyes from the view but was instantly captivated by the clear, greenish blue ocean that stretched as far as her eyes could see.

"Yes. Get up," Dominique reiterated. "We've got things to do, sexy, and there's no time to waste."

Frowning, Ciara fanned her unruly hair out of her eyes and shook her head at the smiling face before her.

"Dominique, I need just a little more sleep. Then I'll be ready, all right?" She tried to buy more time.

"Nope. It's not all right." Then folding his arms across his broad chest and smiling even brighter, he added, "I'm ready to hit the slopes, so you have exactly one hour to get your cute little ass ready."

"Slopes? What the hell are you talking about? As tired as I—" Ciara began, only to be silenced by Dominique's next move.

Snatching the covers from the bed and Ciara's naked frame, he bit his bottom lip and shook his head at the mouthwatering yellow body that lay spread eagle before him. Though he felt an instant stirring in his groin at the sight, the memory of the many hours of sexual bliss they had shared the night before, along with the realization that he would be unable to quench his thirst quickly if he acted on his feelings now, caused him to put any sexual inclinations on the back burner . . . for the time being. Lifting Ciara from the bed with obvious ease and ignoring her pout and whining pleas, he carried her to the bathroom and tub already filled and awaiting her.

She inwardly smiled at his actions and put up a slight struggle just for the sake of doing so. But in her mind, she realized that even if she did want to comply with his every command, female protocol stated that no man wanted a woman who was weak and unprepared to put up an occasional fight. So, as her body sank into the heated water saturated with aromatic therapy salts, Ciara popped her lips and rolled her eyes skyward, trying to keep up the façade of anger.

Peering down at his watch, Dominique announced, "Okay, Ciara. I'm giving you one hour to get ready. If you're not ready by then, I'll spend the day alone or with Zu-hari and Amnesia. You hear me?" He silently laughed at the look of alarm on her face and barely made it out of the bathroom before hearing the heavy bar of soap hit the door. However, the loud curses that followed let him know that she was by no means feeling the choices she'd been given. Yet, all else aside, as he walked through the suite whistling, he had no doubt that they would be embarking on the day's events in another fifty-eight minutes.

Chapter 39

"Yo, Tremaine, on your word, did Dominique really say we should handle that shit without him, shawty?" Treon asked the question with a look of doubt on his face. However, the look he wore reflected the ones worn by Pimp and Money as they awaited Tremaine's response.

"Psst, that's my word, shawty. Yo, why would I . . ." Tremaine halted his response long enough to allow the waitress to place their drinks on the table and leave ". . . bring you niggas a load of bullshit? Come on, now. We've been doing this shit for too long to get cold feet now. What, have you all got soft on me now that you're rich?" He eyed each of his partners with questioning stares as he downed a straight shot of vodka and lime.

"Yeah, we're all soft now, muthafucka. You're a silly-ass nigga, man. Damn," Money exclaimed, shaking his head.

"Yo, chill, shawty," Treon said flatly. "Tremaine, all we're saying is we've never made any moves like this without Dominique. You already know that each of our hearts pumps nothing but ice water. But doing anything this serious without the whole team could be catastrophic."

"He's right," Pimp chimed in. "Rolling without Dominique just doesn't seem logical."

Exhaling, Tremaine allowed their points to sink in before revealing the one aspect of his scheme he had held back in case they were reluctant to go along with his wishes. "Look, I don't know about the rest of you, but

I'm not letting over $6 million slip from my grasp." The sudden looks of greed that replaced their previous doubtful looks made it clear to him that his three cohorts had a change of heart. So, although the vote hadn't been tallied yet, the upcoming heist had pretty much been agreed upon.

Everything was moving along as expected, and thanks to Dominique's ability to remove his nosy girlfriend—the federal agent from Atlanta—no one could have been happier with the situation than the older, cultured gentleman who sat behind the antique mahogany desk. That level of exuberance led the man to remove a gold box from his desk drawer and extract one of his prized possessions. He placed the finely rolled cigar between his thumb and index finger, thinking not for the first time that much care and hard work had gone into the completed product in his grasp. Yet, he also realized that with all the security that blanketed the country after the World Trade Center attacks, the days of receiving bulk loads of illegal goods through customs were a thing of the past.

Meticulously preparing the cigar, he snipped the end and ran the tobacco beneath his nostrils to bask in the scent before placing the tip between his lips and using a gold and emerald-encased lighter to spark it. Then closing his eyes as he inhaled the pungent aroma, he slowly exhaled, allowing the smoke to waft toward the ceiling. This was the ritual he used each time he smoked one of his priceless Cuban cigars.

"Sweetheart, are you coming to bed?" the man's wife questioned, disturbing his occupied mind.

Holding his woman with an unblinking stare, the man paused, thinking, *God, she's beautiful.*

"What?" She blushed, allowing her balance to shift from one stiletto heel to the other. While doing so, the slit in the front of her sheer gown revealed an abundance of creamy thigh.

"It's nothing," the man answered, averting his eyes from his wife's stockings and garter belt. "I was just marveling at how beautiful you are and how lucky I am to have you," he informed.

"That's so sweet, darling." Her blush deepened even further. Then flashing him a longing look, she repeated, "Are you coming to bed?"

"Not yet, honey. I need to make a very important call, but I promise you it won't be much longer, all right?"

"Okay," she replied. As she turned to leave, the displeased look on her face clearly showed that his answer was far from okay. However, playing the role of a dutiful wife and playing it well made it impossible for her to voice her true opinions on their marriage, or for better words, their *lack* of one.

Watching his wife until she exited his study, the man stood and walked across the room to lock the door. He needed the utmost privacy to make the call that could make the difference in whether they all continued to grow and prosper—or failed. Removing the receiver with the thought that failure wasn't an option, he punched in the numbers he'd memorized and waited.

"Yeah?" a gruff voice stated flatly on the other end of the phone.

Wincing at the tone and generally unprofessional manner that the man had used, the man momentarily held his planned response.

"Hey, is this the big guy?" the gruff voice questioned.

"Umm . . . Yes, this is he," the man replied in perfect diction, more for sarcastic purposes than anything else. He held a low opinion of illiterate individuals.

"Well, I would love to hold a long, drawn-out conversation with ya and all, but it's late, so—" the voice began.

"I agree," the man said, cutting into the gruff voice's words. "It's a go on this end, and I don't expect to have any mistakes on your end. My fee is 50 percent of the take, and I'll forward all my offshore account numbers along with the remainder of the information as soon as we disconnect our call. Now, do I make myself clear? Because if you don't understand me now, there will be no second chances."

"Yeah, you're perfectly clear. There will be no mistakes. And after this job, I hope we can work together more in the future."

Smiling to himself, the man known as the "big guy" said, "How about we get this job out of the way first? Then we can deal with the future as it arises." However, what he really wanted to say was, *If everything goes as planned, in thirty-three hours, I'll never have to work with your ass again.*

He had played the game long enough, and the time had come to tie up all loose ends. No one would be safe from his mighty wrath when it was all said and done.

Chapter 40

Though Ciara couldn't have begun to fathom how they would find any ski slopes, much less any that would have snow for them to ski on, to her utter surprise and true to his word, Dominique had done the impossible. He had truly whisked her away from the unbearable midday heat of the desert and delivered them to the wintry climate of a 180-meter indoor ski facility. Even after discarding their summer outfits for heavy snowsuits, skis, and goggles, she was awash in total skepticism as she gawked through the blizzardlike setting at the exact replica of a ski resort. Snow-covered trees, ski lifts, and snowmobiles abounded for as far as the eye could see. But the most unbelievable thing was that this fantasy creation was only one of the many attractions housed inside the Mall of the Emirates, which was acclaimed to be the "World's Largest Mall."

Lowering his goggles over his eyes, Dominique interrupted Ciara's chain of thought. "A'ight, you claim that you're nice on these," he said, nodding down at their skis. "So, how about we place a small wager on the outcome of this little race to the bottom?"

Ciara grinned at his suggestion. "So, what's the wager?" she asked, confidently lowering her goggles.

"Uh, let's see." Dominique smiled mischievously. "If I win, you have to give me head on command for a twenty-four-hour period. And if, by chance, you win—which you won't—your wish is my command as well. But if you're scared . . . oh well."

Laughing at his challenge, Ciara dug her poles into the snow and replied, "You say the word, and I'll meet you at the bottom of the course." However, she failed to tell Dominique that when she was a youth and her family was stationed in Europe, Switzerland and the ski slopes they were renowned for had been her family's vacation spot. Not only was she an avid skier, but she also couldn't wait to demand her payment. Unknown to Dominique, as soon as he yelled "Go!" he had already sealed his fate.

Ciara's moans resounded loudly throughout their bedroom. Although her position on top of Dominique's face spoke of her dominance, in all truth, she was at his mercy.

Cupping her soft ass with his strong, veined hands, he pulled her pussy closer to his face, giving his probing tongue the full access he sought. But even as he repeatedly dug into her center, causing her moisture to coat his face, he found it amazing that his punishment for losing the race had really turned out to be his victory after all.

"Ugh-h-h, daddy, I can't . . . take it . . . anymore," Ciara whimpered in a strained voice. Clamping her eyes tightly shut and holding on to the headboard while gyrating her hips trying to dislodge the thick tongue wedged inside her, she couldn't recall anyone ever sampling her juices so thoroughly. In fact, as she encountered her fourth orgasm, which could only be described as mind-blowing, the last thing she could think about before her shrill scream reached her ears was, *Please, God . . . Make him stop eating me like this.*

Inwardly smiling at her outburst, Dominique intensified the rapid flicks of his tongue. But he wasn't through with Ciara by far, and as he clamped his lips on her clitoris and began to suck on the extended, sensitive flesh, her violent shudders and loud cries alerted him that she would more than likely be out like a baby in no time flat. With that thought in mind, he concluded that when he finished with her, he had one more appointment he needed to deal with before the night's end.

Dominique couldn't help but notice the vast multitude of women who had come out to flaunt their beauty for the numerous rich and famous patrons who picked Amnesia as their club of choice for the evening. On second thought, after noting the alluring array of Moroccan girls in attendance, he decreed that his club catered to the most beautiful women in the world.

"I take it that the eye candy is to your liking," Zu-hari said, sauntering up to Dominique.

Returning the mischievous smile reflected on the heavenly face before him, his previous thoughts of the beautiful women around him instantly resurfaced. "Yep, I guess you've figured me out, as usual, Zu-hari."

"That's not so hard to do, you know?" Then flashing him her breathtaking smile, she said, "Follow me so we can go somewhere a lot less noisy and talk."

Dominique followed close on her heels as she walked through the crowded club. Though he caught flashes of the numerous women who tried to gain his attention, for the most part, he couldn't keep his eyes off of Zu-hari's shimmering backside and the gentle flow of her hair as it swept the contours of her tapered waist with her every step.

Tossing a glance over her shoulder, Zu-hari winked her eye invitingly, momentarily letting her eyes linger below Dominique's waist. Then snapping out of her contemplative state, she opened the door to her office and ushered him inside.

Dominique inwardly smiled at the sly look on her face as he passed her and took a seat on the desk. The office wasn't as large as his own, but Zu-hari had furnished it with a state-of-the-art visual surveillance system and ultramodern furnishings.

"Would you like me to fix you a drink?" she asked in a low, sultry tone.

Dominique didn't answer. He chose to appreciate the picture of pure sexuality that Zu-hari embellished instead. She wore a Versace sheath dress that stopped only inches from her knees. But the slit in front nearly stretched up her thighs to where her panties should have been.

Feeling naked under Dominique's gaze, Zu-hari swallowed, cleared her throat, and said, "Do you, um . . . want me to . . ."

"Come here," Dominique commanded flatly.

Quickly doing as she had been told, Zu-hari covered the distance between them and hungrily began to kiss her first real love. With her eyes closed, she could not control her emotions when his tongue and hands began to explore her body. It had been so long since they were together, and neither was prepared to wait any longer.

Chapter 41

Tremaine peered down at his cell phone. It had been vibrating all morning, and with all the activity around him, answering it was the last thing he planned to do. His gut feeling told him that the caller was Dominique, and after ignoring his friend's warning, talking to him at the moment was out of the question.

Tremaine tossed the phone on the island counter in the middle of his spacious kitchen and turned to his crew assembled around him. "A'ight, you niggas ready to do this shit?" he questioned, already knowing that everyone in his midst was prepared.

"You already know it," Money snapped as if he had read Tremaine's thoughts.

Smirking, Tremaine gave him a knowing wink before glancing toward Treon and Pimp. "How about you two?"

Treon fastened his body armor and gave Tremaine a nod while Pimp hefted his Mak-90 assault rifle and forced an extended clip inside, making a loud *"click-clack"* sound. Even in their silence, each of his partners had given the necessary responses.

Grabbing his weapon and checking the time on his Breitling diver's watch, Tremaine's attention was momentarily redirected to their reflections in the huge refrigerator doors. They gave off a menacing picture with the array of weaponry they each held. Even without Dominique overseeing their last-minute preparations, their disguises were impeccable.

Tremaine smiled and said, "A'ight, everybody. Grab your gear, and let's get this party on the road." Then reaching for the keys to the newly painted work van that Treon had picked up from the shop earlier, he added, "In the next thirty minutes, we'll be over $6 million richer."

"Ciara, are you almost ready?" Dominique asked loudly as he replaced the phone.

"Yeah, baby. Damn. Give me a moment, would you?" Ciara stopped packing long enough to toss a look over her shoulder at the door that separated the master bedroom from the living room, where Dominique had been pacing back and forth all morning. For the life of her, she couldn't understand what had come over him. But she wasn't about to allow his foul mood to dampen what had been the most fabulous vacation ever for her. Even though they were cutting their holiday two days short for some odd reason, her spirits were still soaring, and she planned to remain that way.

"Yeah, I'll give you a damn moment," Dominique mumbled, getting angrier by the second. Ciara was by no means the cause of his anger, but right now, there was no one else there for him to target since he had begun calling Tremaine. His gut feeling had already raised an alarm in his mind. Now, Dominique was sure that his pigheaded friend had disregarded his warning. He knew without question that his crew could be in big trouble, and he needed to get back to Atlanta ASAP.

Speeding toward the location that the unnamed caller had given, Sabrina was not only excited but also experiencing a nervous anxiety of sorts. There were three other agents in the car with her and another fifteen agents following along with a SWAT unit that specialized in possible hostage situations. Outside of the Academy, she had never experienced any real action. Realizing the seriousness of the situation, she let out a short breath and tried to calm her rapid heart rate.

She was pretty sure that the information the anonymous caller had given was reliable, and from the way they sped toward the scene, she realized that someone in the Bureau felt that it was too. Sabrina was aware that their high-profile case would come to an end very soon. Now, she only wished Ciara was there to share it with her. However, understanding that she couldn't be there, Sabrina redirected her thoughts to the task at hand.

Only a block separated them from the bank they sought, and even though no alarms had been activated, any attempts to call the establishment had come up short. Therefore, they quickly determined that the Metropolitan Parkway branch was being robbed at that very moment, just as the informant had advised.

Like her fellow agents, Sabrina slung her bulletproof vest over her upper body and fastened it snugly as the Crown Victoria came to an abrupt stop. She then attached her thigh holster that contained her Bureau-issued Glock .45 and reached to the floorboard to retrieve the fully automatic M-1 submachine gun that sported an infrared scope. Moving quickly, she dropped one of the extra clips of ammunition she had grabbed in her haste to exit the vehicle to take cover. However, swiftly recovering the clip and scurrying behind the car, the radio of the fellow agent nearest to her suddenly came alive:

"They're exiting the bank! I repeat, the suspects are exiting the bank and moving toward a dark-colored van at the eastern end of the building. Be advised, from our position, it seems that they are carrying assault rifles. Approach with extreme caution."

Sabrina's heart was racing with the knowledge that all her training would be put to the test in the next few moments. She released the safety on her Uzi and raised it over the hood of the Crown Victoria. At the first sight of the suspects rounding the building with their weapons visible and large canvas bags slung over their shoulders, the last thought that entered her mind before the loud clatter of automatic weapons fire erupted was, *It's time to rock and roll.*

Chapter 42

Dominique and Ciara entered the Atlanta International Airport terminal after their long flight. The huge airport was packed to capacity with travelers going or coming from destinations all over the world.

Moving through the airport toward the baggage claim carousel with Dominique at her side, Ciara had a slight case of jetlag, and she found her patience with him waning. She reached out to grab his hand in an affectionate gesture and felt him return the gesture with a slight squeeze of her hand. This caused her to smile brightly, but the sight she witnessed next as she peered at one of the many television screens lining the wall stopped her.

"Baby, come on. We need to grab our luggage," Dominique stated irritably. However, feeling her pull away and rush to the television and newscast playing nearest her, Dominique also found himself drawn to the spot. Staring at the screen with wide eyes, the words that filtered into his ears immediately caused his heart to race uncontrollably as his jaw hung slack.

Ciara stood there, no longer interested in anyone or anything else around her. The only thing that occupied her mind and eyes were the words spoken by the female newscaster who stood amid numerous chalk lines and yellow tape.

. . . We're at the scene of the deadliest encounter between the FBI and any group of armed suspects

in the city of Atlanta. Early this morning, the FBI received information that an undisclosed number of suspects were en route to rob the bank behind me. It appears that these individuals were also tied to many other bank heists that have taken place in the Atlanta area and other vicinities in the last two years.

The four men, whose identities have yet to be released, were killed during a deadly gun battle with federal agents.

We're also sorry to report that six agents were wounded, and two others died at Grady Hospital. Our condolences go out to the families of the murdered and injured agents . . .

Dominique's breath was caught in his throat, and unbeknownst to him, a slight sheen of sweat had gathered on his forehead. As his mind reeled, trying to make sense of what he had just seen on the television, he wanted to scream, *"This shit can't be happening!"* Yet, it was Ciara's loud outburst that snapped him out of his traumatic thoughts.

"Yes! Baby, they got 'em." In her exhilaration, she jumped into Dominique's arms and kissed him. However, upon receiving no response to her actions, she pulled away and stared into his face for the first time since hearing the news. There was a look of hurt she had never seen in her man's eyes before. "Baby, what's wrong?" she asked with sincerity and concern.

Staring down at her with eyes that brimmed with rage and resentment, Dominique's voice cracked when he flatly replied, "I'm going to retrieve our luggage. Grab us a cab."

Ciara was at a loss for words as she watched him turn and walk away. Although she wanted nothing more than to find out what was bothering him and make it right, she could only shake her head in despair as she bit down on her lip in deep thought.

Chapter 43

Arriving at the gym inside the Richard B. Russell Building and surprisingly finding it empty, Ciara quickly changed into her exercise gear. Then she wasted no time in getting down to business.

Thanks to her stress meter registering in the red, which was her explosive peak, and Dominique's mysterious attitude pushing her toward detonation, extreme levels of exercise were the only cure she could think of for what ailed her. Garbed in a pair of spandex shorts, a sports bra, and a pair of Nike Shox, she was going through an array of high-level martial arts moves when Sabrina quietly entered the room.

"Damn," Sabrina muttered in a soft voice just above a whisper as she watched Ciara perform a sequence of punches, kicks, and graceful flips that were nothing short of deadly when used against any adversary.

After completing her moves, Sabrina began to clap, alerting Ciara to her presence. "*Magnifique.* That was truly magnificent," Sabrina stated, adding, "Deadly though," as an afterthought.

"Hey, Brina." Ciara smiled. "I see you received my message."

Sabrina hugged her girl, saying, "I sure did. Now, I'm glad you're home, and I missed you like crazy but don't keep me in suspense. How the hell was your fairy-tale trip to Dubai?"

"Girl, it was beautiful, and I'll fill you in on all the particulars later. But unless you want to fight me right here and now, you had better tell me about the showdown I heard the news anchor discussing as soon as I got off the plane."

Smiling as she weighed Ciara's words, even though she had planned to give her a blow-by-blow account of their shootout, the fact that Ciara held a black belt in karate, judo, and jujitsu pretty much swayed her to forego waiting to tell the story any longer. Sabrina was far from a fool, and fighting Ciara was out of the question because, unlike the many people who didn't know any better, she understood that even though her friend was beautiful, she was the most deadly female that she knew. "Well, since you put it that way, it's a long story, so you may as well make yourself comfortable." Sabrina spoke in a forced voice as if she had been made to tell the story against her will.

Hearing her partner's response and recognizing the humor in her tone, Ciara burst out laughing. Though she had an unbelievable time in the Middle East, and now that they were home, Dominique was weighing heavily on her mind, just to be able to share a moment of jubilance with her friend meant more to her than Sabrina could know.

With no particular destination in mind, Dominique continued to drive through the city and reminisce on the many places and things he and his crew had haunted and done. With misty, bloodshot eyes, it was hard for him to accept that his friends were truly gone and he would never see them again.

Slamming his fist on the steering wheel as a torrent of tears wet his face, he cried out with a sad, wounded voice,

"Why? Man, why the hell didn't you listen to me? You *knew* better, Tremaine. Now, look what the hell you've done."

Pausing his tirade long enough to stare through the tears that stained his face and the rapidly moving windshield wipers, he was surprised to see that his hours of meandering through the city had brought him to the front gate of Tremaine's home. Though he hadn't meant to come here, and he really didn't feel strong enough to look at his best friend's personal possessions and living space, retrieving Onyx and Sapphire while he was there was only right. Pulling to the gate and security keypad by the driver's-side window, he was oblivious to the downpour of rain that drenched him and the interior of the Benz as he punched in the code that he knew by heart.

Watching the gate slide open, Dominique ignored the rain that poured through the open window as he headed up the long, winding driveway and exited the vehicle at the front of the house. The rain mixed with his tears as he took the steps two at a time in his haste to retrieve his girls and be out as quickly as possible.

Using his key, he stormed into the enormous mansion and sharply called out to Onyx and Sapphire. His voice rang loudly throughout the house, echoing from every nook and cranny. It wasn't long before he heard their claws clicking along the shiny marble floor, accompanied by their excited barking.

Sapphire was the first to round the corner and enter the cavernous foyer, with Onyx following closely on her heels. Even in his grieving state, Dominique felt instant elation at the sight of his loyal girls as they jumped up on him in search of the attention that had been absent. However, the rapture he received next was like no other joy he had ever experienced in his 30 years on earth.

"Yo, why the fuck you got to be yelling all up in my crib? And why the hell are you back from your trip so early?" Tremaine snapped, coming around the corner wearing a scowl.

Allowing his tears to flow unrestrained, Dominique wasted no time covering the distance between them and hugging his best friend.

"Nah, man. Come on," Tremaine said, averting his eyes. "You know better than that. I wouldn't have gone against your wishes and done no shit like that." He gave a forced laugh after his lie.

"You have no idea how worried I was when I couldn't contact you. Then when I saw that shit on television, bruh, my heart broke into a million and one pieces." Dominique held Tremaine with an unblinking stare and exhaled before adding, "Man, you niggas are all I've got!"

"Yo, come on with that soft shit," Tremaine said, attempting to lighten the mood. However, as Dominique brushed off his comment and began talking about his trip, he leaned back in his chair as if he were listening, but unbeknownst to Dominique, his mind was replaying the episode that took place at the bank . . .

The Day of the Robbery

"Shit," Tremaine said, slamming his gloved fist into the side of the van. "How the fuck did you not realize that the tire was flat, nigga?"

"Don't ask me no stupid-ass questions! How the hell was I supposed to know that the damn tire was flat?" Treon spat.

"Yo, what the fuck? You niggas gonna stand around and argue the rest of the day or fix the tire so we can go get this guap? You two want the money, don't you?" Money questioned.

Pimp giggled, finding Tremaine and Treon's antics humorous.

Mumbling under his breath, Tremaine was fuming as he returned to his four-car garage and searched for a hydraulic jack. Thanks to Treon's negligence, they would be running every bit of thirty minutes behind schedule.

When they pulled to a stop a block away from the bank, all conversation in the van abruptly ended. What the four passengers encountered up ahead made their blood run cold. Federal agents crouched behind their vehicles, while others carrying high-powered weapons sought cover behind the numerous vacated places of businesses lining the block.

A police officer wearing tactical gear constantly peered over his shoulder in the direction of the bank. Finally, he frantically waved for them to move along. However, at that moment, the bank robbers came into view, and immediately taking notice of their surroundings, they opened fire with a barrage of AK and SK shells. This prompted the agents, who held the upper hand and a superior arsenal, to open fire as well.

"Man, get the hell out of here!" Treon stated in a stunned whisper.

However, rooted to the spot, Tremaine swallowed the bile that threatened to erupt from his throat as he watched the first of the four robbers take several hits to his upper torso. He tumbled backward and fired his weapon with the last of his strength before collapsing in a heap.

Slowly leaving the scene after witnessing more than enough, the four friends held their own silent vigils. After witnessing the ambush that was taking place at that very moment, they each realized that had it not been for the flat tire and the luck of the gods, the four men fighting for their lives could have been them . . .

"Yeah, Dubai was great, and you need to go check out Amnesia as soon as you get the chance," Dominique said, slapping Tremaine on the shoulder and unknowingly luring him out of his deep contemplation.

"Um . . . I'll . . . uh, be sure to do that," Tremaine stammered.

This nigga hasn't heard a word I said. He's probably thinking about a new shot of ass or something, Dominique reasoned with a laugh.

"What?" Tremaine questioned suspiciously.

"It's nothing . . . Nothing at all," Dominique replied. He stood up. It was time to go and make amends with his lady. And now that he knew that his friends were safe and sound, life as he knew it was a beautiful thing once again. Now, he just hoped that Ciara would understand.

Chapter 44

The ringing phone disrupted Dominique's thoughts. "Hello," he said into the receiver.

"Well, if it isn't my young partner and pupil," the caller announced at hearing Dominique's voice.

The word "pupil" and the caller's arrogant tone cut Dominique to the core because he was no one's student or flunky. Speaking in a flat tone, he stated, "Yeah, what's good?"

"What's good? Haven't you heard? I took care of our little problem as I promised, and now it's back to business as usual," the caller boasted.

"I don't know, man—" Dominique began but was quickly cut off.

"That's correct. You don't know," the caller said in a relaxed but authoritative manner. "And that's exactly why I'm bringing you up to speed."

"Bring me up to speed on what?" Visibly irritated, Dominique was ready to end their call *and* relationship. They had experienced a beautiful run, and like all good things, it was time to cut his losses and move on.

"Twelve million dollars, that's what."

"Huh? How about running that past me one more time?" Quickly abandoning his last thought, the astronomical amount of money mentioned was an instant deterrent to any idea he may have had concerning cutting his ties with the caller.

"You heard me correctly. I said $12 million. Now, if you want to hear more, meet me at the Hard Rock Café in two hours. And, Dominique, do be on time because you know how I hate to wait."

"Oh, I'll be there, all right. Just save me a seat." Dominique ended their call and reflected on what he'd just heard. If this information was anywhere near as legitimate as the rest of his inside connect's intel had been through the years, he realized that they were about to hit the mother lode.

That thought and one more devious idea brought the sly smile he now wore to his face. The only thing he bounced around in his head after the concept had come to mind was *How can I eliminate this arrogant son of a bitch and keep his portion of the money?*

The funny thing was, had Dominique read his mentor's mind and truly known the bad thoughts bouncing inside his head, he would have known that the words, "All money isn't good money," rang much truer than he wanted to believe. Because in this case, he wasn't the only one who was scheming . . .

Chapter 45

"Hold on a moment," Dominique said, frustrated with the interference of his continuously vibrating phone. Finally, though he'd ignored it the first two times it rang, having the third ring come so close behind the first and second, and knowing that it wasn't Ciara due to her text message, he grabbed the phone and barked, "Who is it? What do you want? And make it quick because I'm in an important meeting."

"Baby, it's me, and I want to see you more than you know," Olivia said in a troubled voice that cracked with emotion.

Recognizing the caller immediately, Dominique lowered his tone and turned away from his lunch companion and partner of sorts. "Look, I'm afraid this isn't the time for this conversation. As I stated, I'm busy, and I—"

"No, Dominique. I'm not going to allow you to brush me off this time. I love you," she said softly. "And I can't allow you to continue to treat me with no respect or regard for my feelings. Therefore, either you cut the games and love me how I deserve to be loved, or any relationship we once had is over." Sighing, she said, "Now, Dominique, what's it going to be?"

Dominique pushed the "end" button on his phone, switched off the power, and placed the device in his complimentary glass of ice water before retrieving his glass of white wine and returning his attention to his associate, who was making a not-so-good attempt at stifling his grin.

Flashing a no-nonsense look across the table, Dominique thought, *That bitch must have bumped her head, giving me an ultimatum. Maybe she'll get the message when she gives her next proposal to the water.* "I'm sorry about that. Now, what were you saying before we were interrupted?" he asked smoothly, disregarding any other thoughts of Olivia.

Shaking his head, his older associate burst into laughter. "Boy, you're one of the coldest dudes I've ever met. And other than that, the only thing left to say is that I need you and your team to be ready to pull off the last and final job that we will ever need to do." Then peering at his watch, he added, "In another forty-three hours, if everything goes as planned, we should be over $12 million richer."

Giving his associate a brisk nod, Dominique said, "Not only will I second that remark . . ." he lifted his drink in a salute of sorts and continued, "but I'll also toast to it."

Clinking glasses and turning up their drinks, Dominique added, "Okay, now that we've got that out of the way, how about letting me use your phone to call my woman?"

Chapter 46

"Come on so we can find out the results of your pregnancy test," she suggested excitedly, receiving a frown and a sigh from Ciara.

Biting down on her bottom lip, Ciara was even more nervous than she would have imagined before taking the test. Though she wanted nothing more than to be carrying Dominique's child, she realized that if, by chance, the test did come back positive, there was a chance that he wouldn't want her or the baby any longer. There were entirely too many variables to consider if it turned out that she was, in fact, pregnant.

"Come on, Ciara. Damn. The suspense is killing me. What are you going to do, ho?" Sabrina asked, rolling her eyes toward the ceiling.

"It hasn't been long enough yet. You know we have to wait for the process to kick in," Ciara replied, trying to buy more time.

"Uh-uh, bitch. Apparently, you forgot who you're talking to because we both know that more than enough time has elapsed," Sabrina retorted and walked into the bathroom. "I don't know why you're trippin', but if you don't check the results, I damn sure will."

"Brina, don't mess with my test kit. I'll check it myself," Ciara grumbled while following close on her girl's heels as Sabrina lifted the test strip from the granite bathroom counter.

"Oh my God," Sabrina yelled, turning to face Ciara with a bright smile and wide eyes.

"What?" Ciara asked, halting her steps. "What?" she repeated in a louder, more insistent voice. However, as she waited for Sabrina to respond, her heart threatened to burst out of her chest.

Grinning at Ciara's obvious discomfort, Sabrina blurted, "Congratulations, partner. You're going to be a mommy."

Not quite sure of how she felt about the news, Ciara forced a smile and leaned against the door frame. Though she wasn't sure how to react to the news, she did know that telling Dominique was the next thing on her agenda. The thought of that encounter alone caused her heart to race.

"Oh shit. How the hell did you do that?" Dominique questioned in amazement, which caused Onyx and Sapphire to bark at his loud outburst. Marveling at the cordless controls and impressive graphics of his newly acquired PlayStation III game system, he couldn't wait to study every word of the instructions to learn every move the game could perform. Just thinking of all the money he would soon be winning from his partners who hadn't been able to purchase the new system due to it not being available in the United States brought a devilish grin to his face. Finally, it dawned on him that he would have to call his man Itzimotto and thank him for the complimentary PlayStation even if it had run him $1,500 and only cost his Japanese friend $600 in Japan.

"Baby, we need to talk," Ciara said while sweeping an array of newly purchased video games off the couch and plopping beside Dominique. Then giving him a wounded look, she leaned her head against his massive shoulder and heaved a deep sigh.

Onyx and Sapphire each took their places, lying at her feet. This had become their norm, and Dominique began to dislike their being so attached to her. Though he couldn't put his finger on how she had done it, somewhere along the way, Ciara had turned his trained killers into domesticated mutts. "Aye, you two get the hell out of here," he commanded.

The two dogs swiftly stood up, but instead of racing from the room as they should have, they stood in place and looked at Ciara.

Dominique was in utter disbelief when he saw Ciara lower her lids and flick her head toward the open door and hallway beyond, which sent his dogs sprinting out of the room. Giving her a suspicious look, he narrowed his eyes. "Baby, you mind telling me what the hell you've done to my dogs? On second thought, maybe we should give *you* the title of owner since *you're* the only one they listen to," he teased.

"I told you a long time ago that the three of us had a little discussion, and apparently, they felt where I was coming from. Oh, and for the record, they're *our* dogs," Ciara said with a halfhearted smile.

"Humph." Dominique raised his brow and grinned. "I'll have to remember that. Now, on to more important issues. What is it that you would like to talk about, love?" Then hitting the power switch on the game, he gave her undivided attention.

Pausing to arrange her words correctly, the first thing that came from her mouth was, "Dominique, do you love me?" She swallowed, realizing what she had asked because if, by chance, he answered "no," there would be no need even to tell him about the baby. In the seconds that seemed to pass while she waited for his response, their lives together hung in the balance.

"Do I love you?" Dominique repeated the question, giving Ciara a blank stare. "Let me see," he added as if he were juggling the question.

Ciara's heart dropped, and her eyes clouded with the realization that she may have played herself after all.

"Well, do bees love honey? Do cats love milk? Do bears shit in the woods? And do I make you come more than any other nigga you've ever encountered in your lifetime?" Then smiling at how Ciara nodded her head to answer each question, he looked deep into the most beautiful eyes he had ever seen and confessed, "Not only do I love you, Ciara Valentine, but I'm also *in* love with you, baby."

No longer fearful after receiving Dominique's revelation, she kissed his lips softly and whispered, "I love you even more." She then held his gaze and said, "Mr. Dominique Valiant, as of one hour ago, it was brought to my attention that you are going to be a father."

Dominique's facial features were momentarily unreadable. "Are you serious, Ciara?" he questioned and received an affirmative nod in reply. "I'm going to be a daddy, huh?" An answer wasn't necessary. It was a rhetorical question, and he was only speaking out loud. However, the bright smile on his face gave Ciara an indication of his happiness.

"So, we doing this or what?" she mumbled.

"You damn right we're doing it," Dominique snapped. "I wouldn't have it any other way."

It was decided. They were going to be parents. Now, Ciara had to put the second phase of her plan in motion. It was time to call her boss in Washington and talk him into granting her transfer. Then she would need to swallow her pride and kiss Agent Craddock's ass until she agreed Ciara would be a worthy addition to the Atlanta office. After that, their new life would begin.

Chapter 47

"Are you sure this is what you want to do, Agent Valentine?" Agent Craddock asked, leaning back in her big leather chair. Waiting for a response, the senior agent held her with an attentive look.

"Agent Craddock, if I may speak freely, at this moment, there is nothing I want more than this transfer. My life is no longer in Washington. Atlanta, Georgia, and this branch of the FBI is where I want to continue my life and career." Though she had spoken softly, her voice held an unmistakable intensity.

"Is that so?" Craddock smiled, intentionally stalling.

"Yes, ma'am, it is." Ciara realized that Craddock held the power and position to either make or break her at this point, so she took a deep breath, blew it out, and added, "I would also like to take this time to apologize for any indiscretions I may have committed—"

Her apology was cut short by a wave of the senior agent's hand. "Think nothing of it. The fiasco is behind us, and although I order you not to repeat my words, I rather enjoyed your show of spunk. It's not every day that I can arouse an agent enough to see a bit of courage." Craddock then laughed.

Joining in the laughter, Ciara finally began to breathe normally. Foregoing her rigid posture, she allowed her shoulders to slip as she relaxed in her chair.

"Okay," Agent Craddock stated, returning to her authoritative demeanor. "I spoke with your senior agent,

Mr. Johnson, this morning, and he made it perfectly clear that you've got his full support. So therefore, finding that you're held in such high regard in Washington and recognizing your skills myself, I think it's only right that I officially welcome you."

Ciara's smile was breathtaking, yet her voice cracked as she thanked Agent Craddock with all the zeal and sincerity she could muster.

"Yeah, yeah . . . I know," the senior agent replied. "Now, get out of my office. I've got work to do."

"You're right. I'm sorry," Ciara stammered and rose to leave. She had worn out her welcome, but as she exited the office, the only thing that mattered was that she had accomplished the endeavor she'd set out to undertake.

"I'm in place," Pimp said into the mouthpiece that protruded from the apparatus in his ear. Receiving no response or needing one, he removed a pen from inside his sport coat pocket. Instead of using it to write on the deposit slip in front of him, he held it in the direction of the guards, who were positioned around the large bank. Then after counting to ten, which was enough time for the electronic monitors in the van to record the scene, he repositioned the pen to record the area in and around the vault. The pen and miniature camera inside had been obtained while Dominique was on vacation.

"Okay, we got it," Dominique said into his headset. "Make your way back toward the entrance and create a disturbance for the two guards. We'll relieve you in exactly . . ." Dominique hit the timer on his watch. ". . . thirty seconds."

"I'm all over it, boss." Pimp immediately replaced the pen, noted that he now had twenty-two seconds left before the show began, and began to make his way toward the entrance and the guards who stood at their posts. In minutes, he and his crew would be even richer than they already were. With that thought in mind, he headed to complete his task.

Donning their masks and arranging them correctly, Dominique said, "This is the one, men. Nothing we've ever pulled off to this point can compare to the payday that awaits us inside. So, even though I know that you niggas are the best at what you do, I still need to remind you to keep your eyes open. And remember that nothing and no one stands between us from escaping unscathed. It's all about making it home in one piece, baby. Now, is everyone with me?"

Nodding their heads as they hefted their submachine guns and extra clips of armor-piercing bullets, it was more than clear that they were ready for anything short of Armageddon.

Grabbing his own weapon and reaching for the door handle, Dominique said, "Let's rock. Our dough awaits."

"That's right, you bastards. Go ahead and get that money, you greedy, low-life sons of bitches." From where Mr. Douglas sat in his car not far from the bank, he was guaranteed a bird's-eye view of the impending performance. Since he had orchestrated this hit and all the others that Dominique and his crew had carried out, it was only fair that he sat at the helm as the final performance of their careers played out.

Unfortunately, what was not known to Dominique and his cronies was that the ending that they sought, filled with riches, sun-kissed beaches, and the most exotic females on the planet at their sides . . . would not be possible. Instead, thanks to their leader, Dominique, and his unrestrained sex drive, they would each experience doom.

With the small business card in his hand that Agent Ciara Valentine had given him weeks before when they dined at Shady Grove Country Club, it was not only funny, but it was also ironic that Dominique's girlfriend would be the one to bring his enemy down for him.

With that thought in mind and the recollection of how much and how long his marriage to his childhood sweetheart, Olivia, had suffered due to Dominique's selfish and disloyal ways, Mr. Douglas reached for the burner phone that sat on the passenger seat and punched in a series of numbers. Then hearing a female voice pick up, he muffled his voice and spoke into the receiver. "Agent Valentine, I have some information for you . . ."

Navigating through the congested morning traffic, Ciara was euphoric. She was carrying the child of the man she loved. He wanted the baby just as much as she did, and as soon as she returned from Washington with the remainder of her possessions, they planned to begin their new lives together.

Smiling brightly as her heart burst with joy, she began to plan every aspect of her future, even as far as a wedding. She knew it would only be a matter of time before Dominique proposed to her. Getting lost in thought and realizing that she just might have been jumping the gun, she mused whether they had agreed to a commitment. But there was nothing wrong with being prepared when the time arrived.

Feeling the vibration from her phone on her hip, she was lured out of her thoughts. "Hello. This is Agent Valentine speaking."

"Agent Valentine, I have some information for you."

Ciara lowered the volume on the stereo so that she could hear the caller better. Unfortunately, the voice was somewhat muffled, making it hard to understand. "Excuse me, but could you repeat that, please?"

"Am I speaking with Agent Valentine?" the caller inquired, sounding irritated.

"Yes, this is she. Who am I speaking with?" Ciara instantly picked up a vibe that the caller wouldn't disclose his identity. His next words quickly confirmed this.

"Don't worry about who I am. Just listen closely to what I'm about to tell you. Do you hear me, Agent Valentine?"

"Yes . . . um, I hear you." Ciara pulled her car to the side of the street and parked it. For some reason, she felt that the caller deserved her undivided attention.

"The four men that the FBI killed a few days ago in the shootout that's been all over the news aren't the men responsible for the rash of robberies plaguing the city."

"But we caught them red-handed—" she began.

"Look," the caller said sharply, "do not interrupt me again, Agent Valentine. Now, as I was saying, your people killed the wrong men. The men you've been looking for are in the middle of robbing the Atlanta Savings and Loan Bank downtown as we speak. This is not a game, and if you hurry, there just might be enough time for you to catch them."

Ciara heard the caller disconnect and momentarily sat still. With the phone still held against her ear, she was uncertain how to proceed. However, the words "Atlanta Savings and Loan" stirred her from her uncertainty. Only four blocks separated her from the supposed crime scene, and if the caller were credible, it was her civic duty to check into the claim and apprehend the suspects, if possible. Thus, taking a deep breath and pulling back into traffic, she punched a series of numbers into her phone and spoke to the FBI switchboard operator. "This is Agent Valentine, and I'm en route to a possible robbery in progress at the Atlanta Savings and Loan. I'm unsure of the exact location, but backup is needed ASAP."

"Units are on the way. And Agent Valentine, please be careful."

Sighing, Ciara replied, "Let's both hope that backup arrives in time for me not to have to worry about being careful." With that said, she ended the call and raced up the street.

Nearing the entrance and the guards that stood nearby, Pimp glanced at the time on his trusted Breitling diver's watch that they each wore when it was time for business and saw that only ten seconds remained until showtime. He knew that his people would be storming into the bank in a matter of moments, so, taking a deep breath and quickly exhaling, he took one more step and collapsed only mere feet away from the closest guard, garnering his immediate attention.

"Sir, are you okay?" the burly, middle-aged officer asked while hurrying to Pimp's side and dropping to one knee. Receiving no response, he grabbed the shoulder of the seemingly unconscious man and turned him over while calling out to his partner for help. However, when the guard's eyes met the fiery red slits that reflected back at him, he never even blinked when the bank's double doors were thrown open and loud commands to "Get down!" reverberated throughout the cavernous lobby. The .50-caliber Desert Eagle that pressed into his rib cage held his undivided attention.

Placing a chain around the entrance door handles and stationing himself where he had an unobstructed view of the street and bank patrons scattered all over the floor,

Money tossed Pimp the extra H&K MP5 submachine gun that he'd brought along. He watched as the two guards were quickly bound and gagged. As expected, they hadn't put up the slightest bit of struggle, but who would expect them to, with all the firepower trained on them? The robbers had entered the bank and had the scene under control in under thirty seconds.

As usual, Dominique's adrenaline was racing. Moving with an insistent stride, he called over his shoulder, "M and P, you two hold the lobby down. T and T, come with me." There was no need to call their names because, as Tremaine and Treon stepped beside him, it was more than evident they knew the drill by heart. But as Dominique scoured the floor and passed over each employee and patron alike, it wasn't until his eyes locked upon the person that he sought that he came to an abrupt stop.

Seeing the gorgeous Spanish woman cowering on the floor, Dominique instantly recognized her. Not even the long hair partially covering her face could disguise her prominent sun-kissed features. "Mrs. Kaiser," he announced, receiving no response. "Mrs. Christy Kaiser, no one will hurt you, but you must come with us." He spoke tenderly, but his words left no doubt that he didn't plan to repeat himself. He extended his free hand to assist her in getting up, but he wasn't surprised when she peered up at him and accepted his aid.

Now that finding the bank manager had been easy, he only hoped that reaching the safe and the contents inside would go as smoothly.

Though her heart rate hadn't entirely returned to normal in the face of the challenge she now faced, Ciara's nervousness subsided upon arriving at the Atlanta Savings and Loan. Instantly eyeing the bank's entrance and hoping to see some movement inside, after a few moments of nothing, any hope she may have harbored swiftly dwindled.

Inhaling, then quickly releasing the air from her lungs, she opened her door and headed to the trunk in a low crouch to the arsenal that was inside. The last thing that she wanted to do was give up her element of surprise. Doing a mental inventory of what her trunk held, the thought alone gave her that much more confidence to face whatever adversaries exited the bank with the courage and bravery she had been trained for. Even though the odds were far from in her favor, she would prevail. Backup would soon even the playing field . . . at least that's what she thought.

The slender, blond female who couldn't have been any older than her mid twenties should have been smarter than she now showed herself to be. Yet, from his peripheral field of view, Pimp couldn't believe that someone so pretty could be so stupid. As he made his way farther into the lobby, he inwardly smiled at the sight of her wiggling across the carpet to get near what he expected was an alarm. Failing to look behind her and somehow wrongfully gauging his position, she threw caution to the wind, jumped up, and made a mad dash for the desk.

Racing behind her and grabbing a handful of her long, blond tresses, Pimp yelled, "Whoa, hold up, shawty. What are you doing?" he slammed her headfirst into the desk.

"Ugh-h-h!" was her only response. Then unconscious, she crumpled to the floor in a heap, her beautiful blond hair streaked with red.

Seeing her predicament, Pimp cringed at the sight of her wound. Yet, to stop her from pressing the silent alarm button, it was only natural that she received such a punishment. However, hearing Money's loud laughter behind him farther down the corridor, Pimp tossed him a threatening look, frowned at the still body lying at his feet, and went back to patrolling the lobby.

So far, except for the pretty, white employee's senseless actions, their scheme had gone off without a hitch. But as Pimp continued his rounds with his weapon locked and loaded, he peered down at his watch and noticed they had already been inside the bank for over three minutes. For them, this wasn't just unusual; this was unheard of. Glancing toward the vault, he couldn't help wondering what was taking so long.

Lifting the heavy bales of money and placing them in the spacious gym bags, Dominique hurriedly moved through the steel-encased vault like a blur. They were on the clock, and when in situations such as the one that they now found themselves in, time was one thing that one could always count on not to be on their side. However, even as they packed the gym bags, it was painfully clear that the vault housed nowhere near the $12 million that they expected. That alone was reason for alarm. The more Dominique thought about the misinformation he'd been given, the more he began to have a bad taste in his mouth.

After replaying the dilemma in his mind, it dawned on him that it was impossible for someone who had always been on point to the last penny to come up millions of dollars short. It was a setup, and the epiphany hit him with the force of a wrecking ball. "Shit," he exclaimed, halting Tremaine and Treon in midmotion. Though the statement came out in a whisper, the words, *That muthafucka set us up,* reverberated through his head.

"What?" Tremaine and Treon asked in unison.

Dominique shook his head furiously as the truth sank in. "Yo, grab what you got. We've got to get the hell out of here." As he hefted his bag over his shoulder, his first thought was to start murdering employees and patrons alike. But as his suddenly cold eyes met with those of the beautiful Spanish manager staring back at him with fear, he instantly erased that thought. Instead, as they ran from the vault leaving the manager bound and gagged, they only wanted to make it out of the bank with their own lives intact.

Glancing over her shoulder again in the hopes that the cavalry would be pouring around the corner to save the day, Ciara was once more left with the bleak realization that, for the time being, it was just her against the bad guys. So, turning her eyes away from the bank and giving herself the once-over, she saw a battle-ready agent. The FBI emblazoned bulletproof vest and double shoulder harness containing matching Heckler & Koch P2000 SK .40-caliber semiautomatic pistols with insight x 2 laser attachments and the fully automatic UM-15 A4 carbine rifle with scope made her a formidable match for any adversary. Yet, even with all the firepower she possessed, none of her weapons or training could have prepared her for what she saw at that moment.

"Yes, now the party can begin," Mr. Douglas said, sitting up straighter in his seat at the sight of two robbers exiting the bank with their guns swinging at their sides. Though he had no idea which of the masked men was

Dominique, he knew that things would erupt within the next few moments.

Mr. Douglas patiently sat back, watching from a distance as Agent Valentine arrived and set up her barricade. Now, he sat on the edge of his seat and waited for the fireworks to begin. As the first two men reached the car and got inside unscathed, he stared in confusion as two more men exited the bank.

"Okay, Ciara, remain calm, now," she mumbled as she slowly rose above the hood of her car and placed the M-15 in firing position. The last thing she wanted to do was jump the gun, so putting her index finger inside the trigger guard and peering through the scope, she made sure not to tap the hair trigger.

Having allowed the first two suspects to enter the vehicle, she followed the final two robbers through the crosshairs of the rifle's scope. Though each man looked around them as if they were expecting company, neither slowed his stride or raised his weapon. Therefore, Ciara could tell by the confident way they moved that they were professionals. However, as soon as the last two suspects reached the car, all her previous anxiety was erased as she jumped into action.

Rising from behind her car with her M-15 sighted and ready to fire in a hail of death, she yelled, "This is the FBI! Drop your weapons and raise your hands where I can see them."

As soon as the command was given, it seemed as if, on cue, sirens could be heard in the distance.

Dominique was beginning to second-guess his belief that Mr. Douglas had set them up and his decision to leave Pimp behind to ensure that their backs were covered in case they had been trapped. However, hearing the loud command and realizing they had been crossed, he was glad that Pimp was their ace in the hole. But when he followed the voice to its source, in his surprise, he forgot about everything and everyone but the woman standing before him.

"I said drop your weapons and raise your hands in the air! And I don't plan to repeat myself." Ciara was no longer nervous; she was dangerous.

Allowing his weapon to clatter to the ground, Dominique turned to Tremaine, who wore an incredulous look, and said, "You heard her."

"Man, are you crazy?" Tremaine mumbled, hearing the sirens and looking around nervously.

"I got this," Dominique informed his friend and partner before adding, "You two toss your weapons out too."

Though Ciara couldn't make out their words, something about the leader's voice gnawed at her insides. What was it about that voice that had somehow thrown off her concentration?

Turning to face his woman, Dominique enacted the boldest move he could to save them all and still live happily ever after. He removed his mask and openly displayed Dominique Valiant before the world.

Gasping at the true identity of the suspect and realizing the lies that she'd been subjected to, for the first time in her life, Ciara found herself torn. On one end, there was her job which had always meant the world to her. On the other end, the man she loved and adored, her unborn child's father, and the love of her life stood before her. Though it should have been as easy as lowering the rifle and walking away, it wasn't that simple for some odd reason. The tears that suddenly clouded her vision were warranted, and as they poured down her face, she could neither hear the sirens nor Dominique's words through the sudden throbbing in her head.

"Baby, put your weapon down," Dominique stated softly, soothingly. Though the sound of the sirens was nearing and the situation was becoming direr by the second, it seemed he was in complete control of the predicament they now found themselves in.

Shaking her head as the tears cascaded in a relentless torrent down her face, Ciara was by no means denying Dominique's request, nor had she heard it. Instead, she was trying to come to terms with the decision she had just made.

Slowly lowering her weapon as she held Dominique's stare, she realized that regardless of the repercussions she may have to endure if the Bureau found out what she was about to do, there was no way in hell that she could allow the most important man in her life to spend the remainder of his life in a federal prison. Mouthing the words, "I love you, Dominique," she exhaled. Then noticing the smile that lay just below the surface of her man's face, she allowed her trigger finger to slip from its position on the trigger and gave him a forced smile of her own. She thought that he would have to stop this madness so that they could start their family on a positive note.

Suddenly, the look of utter horror that appeared on Dominique's face as he screamed, "No, don't do it, man!" caused her to spin around at the exact moment that a loud burst of automatic weapons fire reached her ears and peppered her body.

The pain that ripped through her stomach and chest as she crashed into the freshly paved asphalt proved that she had really been shot, and it wasn't her imagination.

"No-o-o-o! Ciara!" Dominique yelled while running to where his woman lay covered in blood. His friends could only stare with defeated looks on their faces. Pimp shook his head in despair, yet he had only done what he'd been instructed to do. It would have never happened if he had known that the FBI agent was Ciara.

It no longer mattered because Ciara drifted toward a place where no pain existed. The last words that reached her conscious mind before she drifted into the dark abyss that was engulfing her were, "Come on, Dominique! She's dead, man! Come on, now. We've got to get the hell out of here." Unfortunately, she never saw how her predicament affected the only man she had ever truly loved.

With blinding tears in his eyes, Dominique allowed Tremaine to guide him away. Had he turned his head toward the street at that moment, he would have seen Mr. Christopher Douglas III as he exited.